LAST RESORT

A gripping action-packed thriller

DAN LATUS

Jake Ord Thriller 3

Joffe Books, London
www.joffebooks.com

First published in Great Britain in 2022

This paperback edition was first published
in Great Britain in 2022

Cover art by Jarmila Takač

ISBN: 978-1-80405-122-1

CHAPTER ONE

In the street, he saw a man he recognised and began to sweat. He had seen the man once before, a long time ago, in another place. Now he was here, sitting in an office as he walked past. It wasn't much, but it was enough. He knew how they worked. It meant they were on his trail, and perilously close.

He had to assume he was right about that. To think anything else would be plain foolish. If he was wrong, he would lose nothing of value. If he was right, he risked losing everything.

He chose sensibly, logically. His room, even his hotel, was no-go territory now. He couldn't risk going back there. Not after everything he had given up.

If they did know where he was staying, they would also know about his car. So that, too, would have to be abandoned. He could take nothing with him that he wasn't already carrying.

No use meeting the contact team for the debriefing, either. They would know about that, too, and he doubted the Americans would still be alive, anyway.

He walked on past the hotel where the meeting was to be held, doing some stocktaking and calculating the odds of him making it out of this alive. What had he lost, and what did he still have? Could he survive even, after all this?

His conclusion was bleak. Not alone, he couldn't. Not here. This was a difficult country for him now. He needed help. But from where, from whom? Nobody would help him now, he thought despairingly.

Then it came to him. A phone number provided long ago by a man who had said to call if he ever needed a get-out-of-jail card. Well, now he did.

* * *

So he made the call. And help was offered. Promised even if, some might have thought, a little reluctantly. The relief he felt was exhilarating. It was a time to sink to the ground and kiss the earth with gratitude. Had he been a religious man, he might have rushed to look for the nearest church. As it was, there was no time, and there were many miles to go before he could sleep.

CHAPTER TWO

London, England

With a grimace, Sir Giles Henderson held the phone away from his ear and sighed. He returned the handset to his ear. 'So where is he now?'

He listened to the inevitably complicated explanation while his brain worked feverishly. How significant was this? he wondered. How much did this man matter? Was it worth the very considerable effort that would be involved in trying to save him? And would he be supported, if he put scarce resources into mounting a rescue attempt where the Americans had already failed? Would the Americans mind, even? Perhaps feel slighted? More important than all of that, could it actually be done? Was a successful exfiltration feasible?

All unknowns. More than ever these days. It shouldn't be like this. But it was. They no longer worked independently of government and when the government of the day believed, deep down, that people like him were a waste of time and money, as well as an ongoing potential political embarrassment and an actual cause of trouble, it was risky to do anything at all. Especially with Brexit and its aftermath having overtaken everybody.

Yet the appeal had been made, and heard. A man in extremis had grasped the straw he had once been offered — an extraordinarily long time ago! — and had made the call. So, this was no time to sit on one's hands or look the other way. There was a promise to be kept. And it would be. Henderson prided himself on being a man to whom such things still mattered.

All that said, his resources were very limited. Offhand, who could he spare or call on at a moment's notice to mount such a mission? Nobody, really. Nobody very much, and nobody free. Cypher clerks and information managers — IT warriors — were no good for this sort of thing. Nor were people on trade missions. People in the embassy even less so.

He just didn't have the field officers these days, the men and women immersed in a language and culture who could be called upon when the need arose. Not to spare, at least. Times were hard.

Slovakia might be difficult, too. National sensitivities, and all that. Cultural affinities with Russia. A security clamp-down highly likely after what appeared to have been a failed coup attempt. And, even more important, nobody in place. Somewhere else — almost anywhere else — would have been infinitely better.

Then a possibility came to mind, an inspiration. A name. God knew where it had come from. Was it possible?

He thought and quickly decided it was indeed possible. At least, it might be. A long shot, certainly, but not totally inconceivable.

But where to base the operation, if indeed he was given the go-ahead to mount one? Once again, inspiration rose to the challenge when it was needed. No more than a possibility, again, like the other, but hadn't he always been in the business of clutching at straws? Wasn't that what he did?

The dull plod was for others, not for him. He had always been prepared to take a chance, and his outsiders had a remarkable record of success, even if he did say so himself. And do you know what? he mused with a growing thrill. This one just might fly.

He staunched the endless flow of explanation and self-justification still pouring down the line from a not-very-capable military attaché. Mentioning a specific place, he said, 'Tell your man that if he can get himself there, we'll be able to help.'

'Are you sure?' came the worried response. 'That's four hundred miles away. And I can't go with him. I'm far too busy here. You wouldn't believe the paperwork . . .'

'Just tell him,' Henderson intervened. 'And put him on the train yourself, if you have to, or find a car for him. Whatever. Then it's up to him. We can't do everything.'

'Who will you send?'

'I'll let you know.'

Or more likely not, he thought after switching off the phone. What would be the point? Best to avoid potential sources of further difficulty and embarrassment.

He sat for a moment afterwards, thinking it through. Would the man he had in mind do it? He was certainly capable of it. But would he be prepared to go? Henderson gave a grim smile. He would just have to find a way to make the invitation irresistible. Surely he could do that? A man with all his experience? Of course he jolly well could!

CHAPTER THREE

Budva, Montenegro

They had told him to wait in Budva. So, by car, train and bus, slowly, gradually, he had travelled to the Adriatic coast, always using local transport rather than risking the more obvious express routes and services. There, he waited, emotionally and physically exhausted. He had no option but to wait. He couldn't ignore their advice or defy them. He needed their help. There was no one else he could turn to.

Would they send an assassin from Moscow to kill him? Probably. Possibly by poisoning. It was how they often did things. Ever since the Bolsheviks first arrived on the scene, it had been like that. Someone would certainly come, and why not from Moscow? They could operate here just as easily as back there. This town, this country even, might not be part of Russia formally, but in every other significant sense it was.

His compatriots owned it. He had seen and heard that for himself. The streets and hotels, the shops and restaurants, were full of Russian speakers, mostly ordinary people on holiday, but amongst them, inevitably, there would be those who were not. He knew how it worked.

True, some of the people he heard talking in his own language might actually be Montenegrin, but probably not many. Locals would know and speak Russian, but amongst themselves they would use Montenegrin. Besides, there were so few of them — a mere 650,000 people in the entire country — that they were probably outnumbered almost everywhere, and certainly along the coast during the tourist season. All of which made him wonder what he was doing in this place. Why had he been told to come here? It made no sense to him.

He stubbed out his cigarette, and then promptly lit another. When he realised what he had just done, he stubbed that one out too. It crept up on you, the old habit, when you were somewhere where smoking was still a natural thing to do, unimpeded by fanciful Western notions of healthy living. Healthy living was only a valid concept when you had a life expectancy to justify it. He didn't. He knew that and didn't mind. So long as he could do what he had long wanted to do, it didn't matter.

He should never have come here, though, he thought morosely. He was supposed to be safe in this hotel, but it didn't feel like he was. Not during the day, and even less at night. Constant vigilance was required. He was exhausted, but still couldn't sleep much. He didn't dare.

When he did sleep, it was after it became light in the morning. Between then and breakfast time. There were people about at that time, even though the day hadn't really begun, and somehow it felt less dangerous to go to sleep then. It was as if terrible things didn't happen at the start of a new day.

It was nonsense, of course. Assassination teams were not clock-watchers. They were people-watchers, dedicated to monitoring people just like him. They did their work when it best suited them, whatever the time of day. Just as they had in Slovakia. They had hit his contact person from the US Embassy in the early afternoon, and would have killed him, too, had he been there. So, no, he didn't feel safe — and knew he wasn't — at any time of day or night, particularly in this town amongst so many of his fellow citizens.

* * *

Later, he went out, regardless of his concerns. He simply had to. The four walls of his room were becoming too oppressive. He left the hotel and headed towards the town centre, using a pedestrian tunnel that had been dug through the rocky headland that stood in the way. A corkscrew road wound its way over the top of the headland, but that wasn't a sensible or safe option for a man on foot. Without a footpath alongside it, the narrow road was fenced in by steel safety barriers. It would be the easiest thing in the world for a truck driver to inadvertently — or deliberately — squash a pedestrian against the barrier, or flip him over it into the abyss. The pedestrian tunnel was the only sensible way to go.

He was well into the tunnel before he really thought about what he was doing. Then it occurred to him that he was being extremely negligent, stupid, even. In here, he was alone and out of sight. And utterly defenceless. He stopped to listen, struggling desperately to ward off a mounting panic attack. All he could hear was the harsh, rasping sound of his own breathing. Nothing else.

The tunnel was long — several hundred metres — and it had been built in a curve, an arc, that made it impossible to see very far either ahead or behind. He stood still. He wanted to move, and knew he should move, but he was paralysed by indecision. Should he carry on or go back? His pulse rate rose and his heart began to hammer against his chest. He felt sick and about to vomit.

The limestone walls glistened and gleamed in the eerie light from the safety lamps embedded in the rock. Looking back, he could see patches of shadow worryingly capable of concealing an assassin. He was even more concerned by the thought that someone might have followed him into the tunnel and still be hidden by the curve. Just as bad, even worse, there could be someone ahead of him, lying in wait.

Oh, what a fool he was! he thought despairingly. What was he doing? Why did he come here?

He steeled himself to listen intently, but it did no good. The rock walls deadened all sound. There was nothing to be heard from the road high overhead, or from either end of the tunnel. No pebbles slithered or fell. The limestone was solid and unbroken. It was also bone dry and utterly devoid of moss and algae. No water dripped. There was nothing to be heard at all.

Not until he heard the footfalls of someone entering the tunnel behind him.

CHAPTER FOUR

London, England

'We want you to bring him out,' Henderson said.

'Me?'

'You're the best man for it, Jake.'

'How the hell do you work that out?' Jake Ord asked with a chuckle.

Henderson got out of his chair and moved across to the coffee machine he'd recently installed in his office.

'Americano suit you?'

Jake nodded. 'Anything. Why me?'

'Apart from the fact that you're still on the payroll, you mean?' Henderson poured two cups of coffee. 'Well, sort of on the payroll, that is.'

'Sort of is right! I'm a pensioner, and have been for several years. I quit, remember?'

'Hasn't stopped you being active, though, has it? I was impressed with your performance against Fogarty — our law-and-order forces found him impossible to keep, even when they finally caught up. Portugal, Central Europe, Greece — and so on. Some chase!'

Jake scowled. 'I was just responding to events as they happened. Fogarty was trying to kill me, along with others — and damn near succeeded!'

'Even so,' Henderson said, as if to say he knew all that and it didn't make any difference.

Not much escaped Giles Henderson's attention, Jake acknowledged. Not when it came to operatives, current and past. Once he'd got the top job, he would have made it his business to find out all about them all — and then to keep tabs on each and every one of them, including those he had never actually managed or run.

'This is why you called me in?' Jake stirred his coffee vigorously.

Henderson, stirring his own coffee more carefully, nodded. 'Pretty much. We're not over-endowed these days with people with extensive field experience, like your good self. Plenty of computer geeks, of course — and we certainly need them. Lord, how we do! Cybercrime,' he added with a shudder. 'Online spying.'

Not like the old days, Jake thought with amusement. But he knew it was a performance. It suited Henderson to play the elderly buffoon, but he had the sharpest brain Jake had ever encountered. Lightning fast, and then some. You had to be careful playing with Henderson, or you'd lost before you knew the game had even begun.

'Surely you must have people better qualified than me for this job?'

'Not many.'

'But some?'

'One or two, perhaps,' Henderson admitted with a roguish grin. 'If I could find them, and if I could spare them.'

'Well, then?'

'Horses for courses, Jake.'

What did that mean? Jake thought for a moment and then shook his head. 'Where is he, this character? You haven't said.'

'Budva, Montenegro.'

'Montenegro? For God's sake! I've never even been there.'

'Precisely. That's one of your many qualifications for the job.'

Jake was annoyed now. He'd been dragged all the way to London for this?

'I'm not interested,' he said flatly. 'All I want to do is get on with rebuilding my cottage in Northumberland.'

'Ah! Well, there may be a problem there.'

'No, there isn't!' Jake snapped. 'I've got planning permission, a building inspector's approval and every other kind of permission I need. I've also got the money. And the builder has started work, or he should have done by now.'

'Oh, no! That wasn't what I had in mind at all.'

'What, then?'

'Your lady friend. That's what — or who, rather — I had in mind. She's the problem, the potential problem at least, isn't she?'

Jake stared, astonished that Henderson even knew of Magda's existence.

'What the hell are you talking about? In what possible way could she be a problem?'

'Well, Brexit looms, doesn't it? The end game, I mean, now it's actually happened.'

'So?'

'It leaves your lady friend, a Czech or EU citizen, on the wrong side of the border, doesn't it?'

'Like a few million others!' Jake laughed, feeling relieved now. 'Anyway, the prime minister, just like the last one and the one before that, has made it clear that EU citizens living here are to be respected and permitted to stay.'

'Some more certainly than others,' Henderson said with a judicious purse of his lips. 'Those with a criminal background, for example, may well be thought undesirable, and inadmissible. Or un-retainable, perhaps I should say.'

'What's that got to do with it? A criminal . . . ?' Jake stopped and stared, aghast.

Henderson nodded and managed to look a shade regretful. 'The lady in question was, and is, I regret to say, known to the authorities — both in Prague and here. Then, again, her more recent involvement in the sale of a stolen Picasso painting is rather . . . murky, isn't it?'

'It wasn't stolen.'

'Perhaps not — not recently, at least. But it wasn't hers either, was it? I imagine inquiries to establish who it really belonged to — legally, I mean — could take an absolute age. Years, certainly, if not decades. And who knows what might come into the light of day during that investigative process?'

Jake was silent now. How could Henderson possibly know so much?

'However,' Henderson said with a gentle smile, 'I am happy to tell you that we may be able to help. We do have discretion, and a certain leverage, with regard to such matters. Ministers have special powers, you know.'

Jake sighed. The game was over already, and he knew he'd lost.

'So, that's how it is?'

'Indeed.'

'She is the holder of a British passport, you know. You do know that, don't you?'

'Yes, but how authentic is it?' Henderson asked, his eyes twinkling now, as if to say that was the funniest thing he'd heard all day.

Jake was well and truly cornered, and he knew it.

'Shall we continue?' Henderson asked politely, and with quiet satisfaction.

Jake yawned and nodded. 'Might as well,' he said. Then he sighed and added, 'So, who is this guy? And why Montenegro?'

CHAPTER FIVE

'His name is Yuri Bortsov, and he's aged forty-one,' Henderson said. 'He's a Russian national who was born in Kursk. All his adult life — that is, all his working life — he has been in the employ of the GRU.'

'A thoroughly professional spy, then. So, is he a renegade, a double agent or what?'

Henderson shook his head. 'Kindly allow me to tell the story in my own way.'

'Sorry, I'm sure,' Jake said, grinning.

'Yes, I'm sure you are. Now, where was I?'

'You were about to tell me something useful, I hope, something to justify you blackmailing me.'

'Tut-tut, Jake! Your resentment is showing.'

'It's not too surprising, surely?'

Henderson reached for his cup of coffee, took a sip, shuddered as if it wasn't what he'd hoped, and resumed. 'One thing our friend was involved in was an attempted Russian-inspired coup in Montenegro. Did you read about that?'

Jake shook his head.

'Well, it failed. People in Moscow were not amused. Partly because of that, Bortsov came under great pressure and appealed to us for help. And now we want to come to his assistance.'

Presumably, Jake thought, because he'd run to escape retribution. It sounded like the old days. Perhaps the Cold War really had started up again. Putin had turned the clock back. How very depressing.

'Is he worth it? I mean, it sounds like an awful lot of hassle.'

'We believe he is worth it, yes,' Henderson said, nodding firmly. 'He has information we and our allies believe will be very useful to us. And that's why we want you to go to Montenegro and quietly extract him.'

'Budva, you said?'

'Yes. It's a seaside resort on the coast. He's holed up in a hotel there at the moment. It's not an entirely safe place, I'm afraid. Full of Russians, actually. So we want you to get him out quickly, as well as discreetly.'

'Holed up in a hotel full of Russians?' Jake said with an ironic chuckle. 'Whose bright idea was that?'

'Mine, actually. I thought it would be the last place his friends from Moscow would look for him.'

Jake laughed now. 'Let's hope they don't play chess as well as you!'

'Indeed,' Henderson said, allowing himself a small smile.

Jake began to think about the mechanics of exfiltration. 'How badly will his ex-friends want him?'

'Very badly indeed, I'm afraid.' Henderson turned serious. 'We believe they killed two members of a contact team the Americans had arranged for him.'

'Ouch!' Jake said with a grimace.

'Quite. That was when we stepped in. We responded to a cry for help. Not surprisingly, the man was desperate.'

That explained a lot, Jake thought. This was obviously an improvised mission at a time when there were no spare hands available. So the net had been cast wide to try to find someone to man it, and he'd been the sucker who got caught.

'I wouldn't fancy flying him out,' Jake mused. 'They'd be all over us at the airport.'

'I agree. Overland would be best.'

'Then what? Where would I take him?'

'That would be up to you, in the short term. It's so diffi-cult for us to keep a secret these days that I would prefer not to use our usual facilities.'

'Got a leak, have we?'

'Possibly.' Henderson's face was grave. 'Look, Jake, I'll be straight with you. I would like you to get him out of Montenegro, and then keep him somewhere safe for about a month while we get our act together.'

'A month!'

'I'm afraid so. I shall need that time to sort something out for him.'

His recruitment to the cause was making even more sense to Jake now. He thought he could see exactly why he'd been singled out for this job. He was off the books and nobody but Henderson was even thinking of him. Ideal for an unofficial job that would have to be run as a private initi-ative without political sanction in case it went wrong.

But he still wasn't having it. Not on Henderson's terms. Oh, no!

'I'm not taking him to Northumberland with me, if that's what you were thinking.'

'Oh? That's a pity. Might I ask why?'

'Because my place there is private. It's got nothing to do with you, or the service, and I intend keeping it that way. I'm rebuilding my cottage, and I want it to stay clean and off the official radar. *Private*, in other words. And that's a red line for me. Be warned!'

'I see.'

Henderson considered for a moment and then asked, 'Is there somewhere else you might consider?'

'Well, there is, actually,' Jake said after a moment's thought. 'Possibly.'

'It should be somewhere you know well, Jake. When you get there, you shouldn't stand out as mysterious new arrivals and invite local scrutiny.'

'I do know it well,' Jake assured him. 'Don't you worry about that. Now let's sort out logistics.'

CHAPTER SIX

Moscow

Amongst his friends, colleagues and underlings, Oleg Blok had long been known as 'The Old Grey Fox'. He knew that. It was a respectful, even affectionate, label he had long worn with amusement, given that his hair had begun to lose its sleek black colour when he was still in his early twenties.

Looking at his reflection in the mirror, though, he wondered if the name had now changed. If not, it should do. 'The Old White Fox' would be more appropriate now. At least he still had some hair, he supposed, although he sometimes wondered if the fashionable bald look might not suit him better. It would make him appear less avuncular, and more like the warrior he had always been until his retirement.

Retirement? he thought with a wry smile. What retirement? It had lasted twelve months. Then the president had insisted he be brought back to deal with the current situation. Until he had met the president to talk about it, he had been inclined to say no. Or at least, 'No, thank you, sir!' But not many would turn down such a request, not after a personal audience with the man who had done so much to retrieve the tattered fabric and wretched reputation of his country. And he hadn't been one of them.

'Come in!' Blok called, responding to the knock on the door of his office.

'Good morning, General. And may I say how good it is to see you back behind your old desk?'

'And good to be here, Boris. Thank you. Good morning to you, too. How are you?'

Colonel Boris Kozlov, his successor as head of department, was a rather dour, and dour-looking, man. He liked to think he ran a perfectly oiled machine, which he actually did much of the time. The trouble was that he lacked imagination and struggled to cope with unfolding events. He was an administrator, not a warrior, and he hated the unexpected. Blok knew very well that was why he himself had been recalled to the colours.

'I am very well, thank you,' Kozlov said. 'But perhaps not as well as you, General. Life in the country has obviously been good to you.'

'Oh, I was getting fat and lazy in my dacha. It was time I did something useful again. So, what have you got for me, Boris?'

'Our man is in Montenegro.'

'Is he? That's interesting. How did he get there, I wonder?'

Kozlov shook his head. He clearly didn't know enough to justify giving a firm opinion. 'We have caught up with him in Budva, on the coast,' he said instead.

Blok paused for a moment, thinking about it.

'So, Montenegro. That's good. And on the coast is even better.'

'With your approval, of course, I will send the team there to finish the job. They should have done that in Slovakia, but . . .' He finished with a shrug.

Blok shook his head again. 'Send a different team.'

'They are good, those boys, General. They made a mistake, that's all, and they know it. They want to correct it.'

'A different team, Boris,' Blok said firmly. 'One with different orders, as well.'

CHAPTER SEVEN

Northumberland, The English Borders

'So it's not over,' Magda said with a sigh.

'Well . . . it depends what, exactly, you mean by "over".'

'I mean you, me, them — all of it! I thought we would be safe here, but they know all about us — everything! It's the same as everywhere else.'

She hated losing control. Jake could see she was in danger of falling into one of those moods where everything was black. He had to stop it.

'Look at it logically,' he suggested. 'What has changed? Not much. Yes, they know some things about us, and they seem to know something about your background. They probably always did. But nobody's going to do anything about it if we cooperate. We will even be protected, and helped.'

He paused and then added, 'True enough, they've thought of me, and found me again, but how difficult could that have been given the Fogarty business last year? Not very, not for anybody wanting to look. We left a trail across Europe, as Henderson pointed out.

'So now they want me to help them out for a month? Well, why not? They'll pay me handsomely, and the money will come in handy. Plus, you'll get clearance and a legitimate passport out of it. That's not to be sneezed at, given that they seem to know about the passports we got from your Mr Phan in Petrovice.'

Magda got to her feet and went across to the window. She stared out of the one room in the cottage that was habitable at present and watched the builder's men fitting window frames to the newly restored wall of the kitchen extension.

Jake waited patiently. He was on edge, but didn't want Magda to know it. Their life together hadn't always been easy, but he very much wanted it to continue. So he waited, and willed her to be logical and not to focus on the interruption to their plans for the summer. Because that's what Henderson's intervention was: an interruption, a diversion, not a setback or an end to them.

They could afford to take a month out. Even more, if necessary. Their not being here wouldn't stop anything. The builders would continue with their work. The rebuild of the cottage would be completed.

More important, realistically, he couldn't afford not to answer the summons. Alienating Henderson was not something he wanted to risk doing, if only because of Magda's status. Besides, being in credit with him could come in useful one day.

'While you were in London,' Magda said thoughtfully, 'Mr Tait and his men fitted felt all across the roof. He says that next week men will come to put on the slates. They will only need a couple of days to do that. Then we'll be . . .' She frowned, puzzled, and added, 'He used a strange word. Weather-something?'

'Weathertight?'

'Yes, that's it! Thank you, Jake. Then we'll be ready for the wet weather they always get, he says, when the school summer holidays start.'

Jake smiled with relief. 'That's good,' he said gently.

'But we still need to decide about the kitchen and the bathroom fittings.'

'Yes, you're right. We must do that.'

She turned and walked across the room towards him, her feet raising dust from the newly installed timber floor.

'But first,' she said with a wan smile, 'we have work to do, don't we? When do we leave, Jake?'

Still smiling, he relaxed further. They were together again, at one with each other. And back in business, it seemed. They would give Sir Giles Henderson the month he had asked for.

CHAPTER EIGHT

Budva, Montenegro

The hotel was what the hospitality industry likes to call a 'modern resort facility'. There were three main buildings in extensive grounds, close to a private beach and the sea. It was owned by an international chain that had many such hotel complexes dotted around the Mediterranean and the Spanish and Portuguese islands in the Atlantic. There were several pools in the grounds, various sports facilities and a number of small bars and cafes. The gardens were immaculate, the well-tended grassed areas studded with palm trees and flowering shrubs.

Jake spent a few hours after he arrived sizing things up and finding his way around. There was a need for speed, but there was also a need to do things efficiently and effectively. Without fuss, too, if possible. He wanted to be sure of his ground before he made a move to contact his man.

One thing that concerned him about the hotel was that it really was full of Russians, just as Henderson had said it would be. They were tourists, for the most part, innocent holidaymakers enjoying themselves. You could tell who and what they were without even hearing them speak. Many of them wore t-shirts and polo shirts with 'RUSSIA' writ large across the front or the back, and in some cases, both, as if they were fresh from attending an international football tournament. The shirts clinched it, Jake thought with a wry inner smile. They were Russians, all right.

The problem was that half the FSB and GRU could have slipped in with the holidaymakers. Was Henderson right to assume they wouldn't hunt here for Bortsov? To hide him in plain sight was a bold and imaginative move, and no doubt it had appealed to someone with a mind like Henderson's, but it wouldn't have been his own choice. This place was too busy, and too full of obvious dangers.

Then again, he thought with a rueful sigh, the man in the field usually saw things differently to his bosses back home. What was new about that?

Jake watched out for people who might not be here on holiday, but without much expectation of success. Generally, the Russians were in either family groups or large parties of young men. The latter were mostly of an age to suggest they were sports teams on vacation. Then there were big mixed-sex and mixed-age groups that looked like old-style works holiday outings, survivals perhaps from the Soviet era.

Montenegro had obviously kept its appeal to Russian visitors, Jake decided, whatever Putin's fulminations about it having joined NATO and looking towards a future in the EU.

So, what about this guy he had been sent to bring out? How happy would he be here in this luxurious resort? Not very, probably. He would be doing his best to keep well clear of people, compatriots or not. As a single man, he would stand out like the proverbial sore thumb. So, he would venture out of his room as little as possible. It would be room service for him, rather than risking meals in the restaurants. A man alone in a place like this would be pretty damn conspicuous.

Before he made contact, Jake wanted to see if anyone else was keeping watch on Bortsov. It didn't look like it, but he needed to be sure. If there had been more time, and the situation less urgent, he might have spent several days doing a recce before he made his approach. As it was, he would just have to do the best he could, and hope like hell it worked out.

Henderson had made it absolutely clear that the ruthless attack on Bortsov's CIA contact team was likely to be replicated here if the hunters caught up with their quarry. He had to get it right, Jake thought grimly. It wouldn't only be Bortsov who suffered the consequences if he didn't.

* * *

As the day wore on, the prodigious beer drinking of some of the all-male parties in the hotel produced ever louder sounds of merriment, as well as predictable casualties. At intervals, shouts and heavy splashing announced that yet another victim had fallen into one or other of the pools. Invariably, that led to a rush of black-suited security guards from all corners of the complex, desperate to prevent a drowning on their watch.

Jake lingered over a coffee on a quiet terrace overlooking the gardens. After just a few hours in the resort, he was getting a feel for the place, and he knew he ought to make his move soon. Hiding in plain sight might seem a great idea to someone sat in London, but for the man doing the hiding, it would be purgatory. From what he'd been told, Bortsov's nerves wouldn't hold out much longer. Jake had to get him out before he collapsed, and before the hunters found him.

A passing security guard paused to gaze down at a mêlée that had formed around one of the pools. Deciding his colleagues had it in hand, he turned to resume his patrol and caught Jake's eye.

Jake nodded, smiled and said, 'They're having fun!'

'Too much fun,' the uniformed guard said darkly. 'They make our work very difficult, especially at night. Always they fall in the pool. Many, many times — and many, many of them!'

'Russians, eh?' Jake said sympathetically. 'They seem to like it here.'

'Yes. They are happy to be here. And why not? Egypt and Turkey are more difficult for them now, because of terrorism and politics, but here is good for them still. They know they are welcome. Russian people are our friends, our brothers. Always.'

And there you had it, Jake thought as the guard wandered away. The facts of life in the Balkans. Here, at least, Russians were welcome. Montenegrins, like Serbs, had always felt close to Russians, and the ancient cultural bonds still endured.

All of which made the recent attempted coup in Podgorica a little strange. Russian-inspired, apparently. But why had they bothered? Surely they could get what they wanted, anyway? Perhaps the president was just too much of an irritant for the Kremlin, like the one in Belarus had been until he lost an election and needed Moscow to support him while he got the result sorted out.

According to Henderson, the attempted coup had been intended to stop the country entering NATO's warm embrace and reaching out to the EU too. Well, the first part hadn't worked out very well. The coup had failed and Montenegro was in NATO now. The wish to be part of the EU wouldn't go away either. It made economic sense. After all, even Serbia wanted EU membership. So, why wouldn't little Montenegro, whatever Moscow preferred?

Still, if the westward-leaning government could be stayed or, even better, reversed, Moscow would be entitled to consider it a good day's work. Better still if, further ahead, a Russian naval base could be developed on the Adriatic. For any or all of that to happen, a different Montenegro government, one leaning towards Russia, would be very helpful.

Jake shook his head. He didn't know how people like Henderson stood . all the geopoliticking. It certainly wasn't for him. He just wanted to get the job done, and then get the hell out.

Time to go, he decided, getting to his feet. He had learned what he needed to know about the hotel, and he didn't want to wait for nightfall. Better to go now, while it was still broad daylight, and drift away while crowds of holidaymakers were milling around the resort. The car he had hired was parked nearby, waiting. All he needed to do was collect his man.

CHAPTER NINE

Budva, Montenegro

It was when he heard someone entering the tunnel that the man knew it was over. He stood frozen to the spot. The tunnel had become a trap. He couldn't go back, and he didn't know what waited ahead of him. Think! But he couldn't. He couldn't think anymore. He was exhausted. No use continuing to hope. He had travelled all this way, taken all those risks, and what good had it done him? It was over, and his dash for freedom had failed.

Panic set in and sweat began to pour from him. Sickened, resigned, he stood still and waited. He just couldn't run anymore. Then he began to shake with fear as the figure of a man appeared, walking steadily towards him. He stood still, locked to the spot. His time had come. There was nothing more he could do. They had found him. What would be, would be. The way of the world.

The man stopped a few paces from him. He waited for the gun to appear, or the syringe, struggling to keep his eyes open and avoid a total, abject collapse.

'Is this the path to Budva?' the man asked in English.

'What?' he replied automatically, in Russian.

It took a moment for the man's words to make sense. 'What did you say?' he asked again, this time in halting English.

'Is this the way to the town centre?'

It was quite clear now. The man had been sent to administer the solution to the problem he had created for them. But not here, not in the tunnel. They wanted to take him elsewhere. They didn't want blood on the floor in such a public place. Explanation might be difficult. Diplomatic incident.

But the English language? Deception, of course. The usual. Create confusion. He knew all about that. He should do. He'd spent much of his life helping to create it.

The man stared, waiting for him to say more.

'Yes,' he said belatedly, in a daze, struggling to get the word out. 'That is what they told me at the hotel.'

'Thank you.' The man hesitated and stared at him a moment longer. 'Are you all right?' he asked. 'Are you unwell?'

'No, not at all,' he stammered. 'That is to say, the heat . . .'

He petered out. Why this torture? Why not just do it and get it over with?

'Is there anything I can do?' the man persisted.

'No.' He shook his head despondently. 'Nothing. You have your job to do. You must get on with it.'

Frightened almost beyond endurance, he closed his eyes and waited. Get on with it!

But nothing happened. When he opened his eyes again, he was alone. The stranger was a receding figure in the distance.

He took a deep breath and scurried back to the safety of his hotel room.

CHAPTER TEN

São Brás de Alportel, Portugal

Magda smiled and shivered with delight when she saw the villa again, their erstwhile home in the Algarve. Its gleaming white walls shone through the surrounding screen of shrubs and trees, and as she opened the old wrought-iron gate, she smiled at the familiar squeal it made. Jake never had got round to oiling it. She didn't mind. They had been happy here. The noise the gate made reminded her of that.

Or had he? She frowned, trying to remember what Jake had said. Perhaps he had oiled the gate, but it had regrown its squeal. They had been away for such a long time, after all, and would have been away even longer if Sir Giles Henderson hadn't appeared on the scene. Their intention had been to spend the entire summer overseeing the work on Jake's ruined cottage in Northumberland. Now here she was back in the Algarve, with very mixed feelings. This was not a normal visit.

She stepped up onto the terrace at the front of the villa and paused to look around before heading inside. The garden looked lovely. Trees and shrubs were flowering, and they had plenty of green leaves too. The heat now was gentle compared with the searing levels it would reach in mid-summer, and the garden reflected that. She liked to be here for the spring — April was the best month of all — when the cistus and the lavender, and so many other wild flowers and herbs, came into their own. But Northumberland, too, in its own way, was rather lovely in spring. All that fresh greenery, and the lambs running across the hills.

With a happy sigh, she shrugged and turned to unlock and open the front door. There was work to be done here too, and a mission to be undertaken.

She just hoped Jake was managing. He should be. She had every confidence in him. The job seemed straightforward enough, although you could never be sure. And the Russians were so terribly effective when it came to clandestine operations. She had learned that early as a young child in occupied Prague. People had walked on eggshells until the Red Army had left the country.

She and Jake had discussed what she should do now. It would have been good to be beside him, if only to share the driving, but he had said he could manage alone. They had agreed it would be better if she came straight here to open up the villa. There was much to be done, preparations to be made, before Jake arrived with their guest.

Plus, of course, she had needed to give Mr Henderson time to obtain a new passport for her, given that the one she had been using was now known by the authorities to be false. Poor Mr Phan, in her homeland! All his artistry last year, when she and Jake had visited him, gone for nothing.

All in all, it had made sense for Jake to go to Montenegro immediately, and to go alone. So now she was here, also alone, but with much to do.

As she moved through the villa, opening doors and windows, switching on and testing appliances, checking the contents of cupboards and drawers, her confidence that their decision had been the right one faded a little. She thought of a number of reasons why it might have been better for her to have gone with Jake.

One was that she spoke fluent Russian. Many Czechs her age did, and absolutely all of them remembered some Russian from their school days. But Jake didn't know any at all — his working life had been spent largely in Arab countries. Not knowing any Russian language might be a significant disadvantage for him now.

Another reason was that it really was a very long drive Jake was embarking on. They had done much of it together the previous year, and it had taken them three days. Admittedly, they hadn't been driving flat out all the way, but this time, the journey would be even longer. Having someone to share the driving with would have been good for him.

Oh, well! she thought with a resigned sigh. Perhaps the mystery passenger would be able to help. She hoped so.

In one respect, at least, she had no doubts whatsoever. She had every confidence in her man's capability. Jake would cope. Whatever happened, he would meet the challenge. They had been through a lot together the previous year, and she knew what he could do.

It might have been a few years since Jake had been active as a spy, or whatever it was that he used to be, but she had seen him in action not so very long ago and been impressed. She knew how strong and resolute he was, and how he could improvise and deal with emergencies when necessary. So she knew he would be fine.

But somehow that knowledge didn't stop her worrying, all the same.

CHAPTER ELEVEN

After the encounter in the tunnel, Jake decided he had to get Bortsov out of there — and fast! The man was near total collapse, his nerves shot to hell. He wouldn't be able to stand much more.

He returned to the hotel by a roundabout route and headed for reception, intending to sort out Bortsov's bill and then collect him. In the tunnel, he had decided to defer introducing himself. The situation had not seemed right. He hadn't wanted to risk shocking and panicking the guy even more. Better to get everything ready first. Then move fast.

Two men were engaged in discussions with the main receptionist when he arrived at the front desk. One was demanding information, seemingly in Russian. The other turned and gave Jake a look of cool appraisal. Jake nodded affably and looked away, patiently awaiting his turn.

The discussion seemed a little awkward, he couldn't help thinking. Not heated, exactly, but it was protracted and distinctly fraught. Information was being demanded from the receptionist that either she didn't have or was unwilling to give, despite being bullied by the guest — if that was what he was. Jake's curiosity was piqued. From the tone of the exchanges, it sounded as if she was being warned, or actually threatened. Perhaps about an adverse report to management. Perhaps about her future in the job.

He wandered over to a nearby sofa and sat down. It looked like it could be a long wait. Nothing he could do about that without creating a scene.

But when he heard the name mentioned that he himself had come to enquire about, he abandoned thoughts of settling the bill. He got up, yawned wearily, stretched and left. Once outside, he turned to his right and walked briskly towards the next building on the site, hoping Bortsov had made his way back to his room.

* * *

'Hello again! I've come to take you away from all this,' Jake said cheerfully.

The man who had opened the door looked surprised, astonished even. 'You!' he gasped.

'Yes,' Jake said with a smile. 'We've met already, haven't we? Sorry for not introducing myself. Look, I've been sent to collect you by the people you asked for help, and I'm afraid we haven't much time. We have to leave right now. Immediately, in fact.'

'But . . .'

'There's no time at all. Really. Let's go!'

'How do I know you are here to help me?' the man said stubbornly. 'How do I know who you are, and who sent you?'

'Ah! You have a point.' Jake grimaced. 'I've been remiss. Does William Shakespeare mean anything to you?'

'Only on Twelfth Night,' the man replied sharply.

Jake nodded. It was the correct greeting code.

'Men, Russian operatives, I think, were asking for you at reception. They'll be here any moment. We must leave — now!'

'I will collect my things . . .'

'There's no time! Leave them.'

33

Jake grasped him by the arm and tugged. Bortsov reached down to grab a plastic bag waiting behind the door.

'Come on!' Jake snapped impatiently.

Bortsov hung on to the plastic bag tightly as he stepped forward. 'It is important,' he said, seeing Jake's eyes fastening on it.

Jake said nothing more. He shut the door and turned to push Bortsov ahead, urging him to move faster. They walked briskly along the corridor and down a flight of steps that led to an emergency exit.

'I have only what I am wearing,' Bortsov complained, unwilling or unable to comprehend the urgency of the situation.

'That doesn't matter,' Jake snapped. 'Don't worry about it.'

He had already noted that the man was adequately dressed in clothes that included a lightweight outdoor jacket. That was good enough for now. Clothes were the last thing to worry about. He was far more concerned about being intercepted and having to fight their way out of the hotel.

'My car is just outside,' he said, to give encouragement.

Bortsov said nothing. Understandably, perhaps. He seemed confused and dazed by the speed of events.

'Come on — hurry up for crissake!' Jake urged.

* * *

They reached the car without incident. Jake installed his passenger and then flung himself inside.

'Sorry about the rush,' he said as he started the engine and got the car moving. 'There'll be time for talk later. Right now, I just want to get us out of this town. It's too Russified for me!'

Bortsov nodded, leaving Jake thankfully free to concentrate on driving.

CHAPTER TWELVE

The main road out of town was a long series of corkscrew bends that took the road up the mountain front facing the sea. Jake drove hard, without crossing the line into recklessness. He worked the gears incessantly and kept an eye on his rear-view mirror. His passenger remained silent, slumped in his seat, sunk in the trough of despond, it seemed. Probably emotionally and physically exhausted.

'You don't say much, do you?' Jake eventually said, beginning to relax now there were no signs of pursuit. He didn't really want to talk, but he did want Bortsov to stay awake in case they had to respond suddenly to something unexpected.

'You seemed not to want us to talk.'

'Fair enough. I didn't back then, but we're clear now, so we can chat. Who's chasing you?'

'That is nothing to do with you,' Bortsov said bluntly. 'Just shut up and take me where you are supposed to take me. That is all. Thank you.'

On the contrary, Jake thought with amused surprise. It was very much something to do with him. But he didn't press the point.

'What do they want?'

'I give you the same answer.'

35

So there we are, Jake thought with a tight smile. Mind your own fucking business!

He tried again. 'What are you running from? What have you left behind?'

'Dead bodies. There was much killing in the place I left.'

With that, Bortsov switched off, turned his face away and gazed fixedly out of the window.

At least it was something, Jake thought with satisfaction. Not much, but he'd got a reaction. That was good. The man was awake and feisty, which was far better than being in a comatose heap. Maybe he was in a bit better shape now than he had been in the tunnel. He certainly hoped so.

Now back to driving, and the road ahead.

* * *

As soon as he spotted the big Merc in the mirror, he focused on it. The Merc had come from nowhere. One minute the road had been empty. Now there was this big silver thing coming up fast. Too fast.

He watched intently, ready to take evasive action, only relaxing when the Merc had swept past and powered on ahead and out of sight.

'He's in a hurry,' he remarked. 'Dinner must be ready.'

His passenger said nothing.

Jake began to feel a little irritated. It was going to be a long journey if the guy maintained this non-communication policy.

Also, they weren't out of the woods yet. Nothing had happened so far but he couldn't really believe they had got out of Budva as easily as that. He needed his travelling companion to be as awake and alert as he was himself. Four eyes better than two, two brains better than one — and relate and talk to each other. All that shit they used to drum into you on training courses. They needed to do it — now!

* * *

Rounding a corner, they suddenly came upon the Merc again. It was sideways on, effectively blocking the narrow road. Jake swore and stamped on the brake.

At the same time, he glimpsed a black car in the mirror. It was pulling out from a clump of shrubs onto the road behind him.

Shit! A trap. But he wasn't going to stop.

'Brace yourself!' he shouted, gritting his teeth.

He changed down and rammed the accelerator pedal to the floor. The engine screamed as the rev counter shot up into the red.

Instinctively, he aimed, rather than steered, at the rear end of the Merc. It would be lighter than the front end. They hit it hard, with a massive jolt and a screech of tortured metal.

Improbably, their little car smashed its way through, spinning the big Merc round and shunting it out of the way. Then they were out the other side — the road ahead clear! The revs picked up again and they shot forward.

But the collision had not been without cost. The windscreen had imploded and the car was full of bits of glass from it. An air bag had erupted to envelop the passenger. And something was making a terrific banging and rattling at the front end of the vehicle. But they hadn't been stopped, and they were slowly regaining speed.

'You OK?' Jake shouted, as he started punching out the remains of the windscreen.

It was hard to tell what, if anything, his passenger said in reply. Probably nothing. He was too busy wrestling his way clear of the air bag.

'It will do no good,' Bortsov said eventually, sounding hoarse and breathless. 'It is futile. They will come again. We must surrender.'

'Fuck that!' Jake snapped.

'They always win in the end.'

'Not this time, they won't.'

CHAPTER THIRTEEN

Moscow

'There are new orders, General?' Kozlov asked a day or two later.

Blok nodded. 'We need to catch him, not kill him. The president insists, and I agree with him. I believe he is right.'

'May I ask why?'

'It is the old way, Boris. How things used to be done in the KGB, as the president reminded me.'

'The KGB?' Kozlov said dismissively.

'Yes. The president's very own, and very valuable, training ground.'

He knew what Kozlov thought about that. The GRU had always regarded itself as superior to the KGB, the FSB, and to all the other intelligence agencies that existed, or had done in the past. At one time, he had shared that view himself, but not now. He couldn't afford to. Nor did he want to hear anything along those lines from any of his staff.

'But if we eliminate him,' Kozlov said, 'the information he has will not reach our enemies, and we make an example of him that will discourage any other traitors.'

'True. But there is more to it than that. There are things we want to know from and about him.'

Kozlov seemed sceptical still.

'Who did he contact, for example? And how? Where and how did they propose to take him? What, exactly, did he offer them, and did they offer him? All those things it would be very useful to know.'

'Before we eliminate him as the traitor he is?'

'Possibly, but perhaps not even then. In the old days, we never acted precipitately. We won't now, either. It may come to that, eliminating him. But before it does . . . Perhaps we should see if we can do better by swapping him for something, or someone, from the Americans. We must be patient, Boris.

'Anyway, enough! The president has made his views clear, and we will follow his instructions.'

Kozlov, of course, said yes. But Blok thought he probably didn't agree. He just wasn't going to say so. He wasn't stupid. A wrong had been committed, and he wanted to put it right. But what was to happen wasn't his call.

In some ways, Blok agreed with him. But the decision wasn't his to make either. The president had made it perfectly clear what he wanted, and the president was an old hand at this game. Besides, only a fool would risk running counter to his wishes. If there was no alternative, Bortsov could be eliminated, but not before that point had been reached. What was needed was a victory on the big stage, not a local settling of accounts.

The president had also made it quite clear that was why he had sent for Blok personally. 'You know this man, General, better than anyone else. So you can understand why I want you to look for him — and find him,' he had said.

It was true, of course, Blok thought. He probably knew Bortsov better than anyone alive. He was the man who had recruited him. So, it was perfectly reasonable that he had been brought back to look for him. Nor had he minded being summoned. Already he had become a little tired of tending his garden. The cabbages and potatoes could look after themselves for a while.

'It would be better if we had no computers,' Kozlov said with a weary sigh, breaking into Blok's thoughts, 'or if we didn't use them.'

'Then information could not be hacked? I agree with you.'

It was true, if irrelevant. Computers were not the issue here.

'The problem, as the president pointed out,' Blok added, 'is that this man has information that is not on the computers. Some is on paper files, in locked filing cabinets, but more, much more, is in his head.'

This won't do! Blok thought with a wince. I'm making the case myself for getting rid of Bortsov, not recapturing him. I can't afford to be doing that. I must be getting old!

CHAPTER FOURTEEN

Jake gritted his teeth, squinted his eyes against the wind shrieking through the gap where once there had been a windscreen and focused on getting the car moving as fast as it was still capable of going. The black car that had sprung the trap wasn't in sight now but it was very much in his mind. He didn't believe he wouldn't see it again.

But first things first. He pulled out a knife and stabbed the air bag. The mass of inflated plastic subsided. More of the passenger appeared.

'You OK?'

The passenger said nothing. He just continued wrapping up the deflated plastic bag and stuffing it down on the floor. It was good to see him actually doing something positive, Jake thought grimly. It made a welcome change.

After a few minutes with no signs of further pursuit, he pulled into the side of the road and leapt out, leaving the engine running, to check the damage. At the front of the car, one end of the bumper was trailing on the road, making a lot of the noise. He kicked it free. There was no other obvious damage to see, thankfully, apart from the smashed windscreen. He scrambled back into the driver's seat and got them moving again.

'That is better,' the passenger said, almost as if he approved. 'Glad you agree!'

It felt like a step forward in their relationship. Jake gave him a grin.

* * *

The black car did not reappear. Other vehicles emerged from the gathering gloom, but they were all coming towards them and seemingly unconnected with the ambush. Jake hoped the fading light was too poor for oncoming drivers to notice the state they were in.

Squinting hard, he ducked his head, trying to minimise the impact of the cold blast in his face and to stop his eyes watering. Goggles, like they wore in the early days of motoring, would have been a big help.

The passenger sank ever lower in his seat and pulled the deflated air bag back up and over his head for cover and warmth.

But there was nothing to be done about the rattling and banging that was increasingly audible over the shriek of the wind. It sounded as if the car was breaking up and coming apart.

What a bloody mess! Jake thought with a grimace. And so it was. But some of the screaming urgency had left him now, and he wondered about what had happened. How the hell had the people chasing Bortsov known where they were? Even if they had been watching the roads in and out of Budva, they didn't know about either him or the car he had hired. So how could they have known he had Bortsov with him?

He had told no one of his route either, let alone when they would depart from Budva. All even Henderson knew was the country to which he intended taking his man, not where exactly or when. As for getting there, well, he hadn't known himself how he would do that. There hadn't been a plan.

Yet the opposition — Russians, presumably — had found them, and had come close to wiping them off the map. It was a worry, a big worry. If they could do that once, they could do probably do it again.

By tracking? Was that the answer? A tracker on the car he had hired?

Some hire cars had them, he knew, to allow the companies that owned them to keep an eye on their property. There didn't need to be collusion with the hire company either. The data, if it existed, would be on a computer, and anything on a computer could be hacked. Was that how it had worked? A commercial tracker system the Russians had broken into?

No, he didn't think so. He shook his head. They would have needed time to identify him to do that, and they hadn't had it. What, then?

Alternatively, Bortsov himself could have alerted them accidentally. A quick phone call intercepted. Or even just a phone they knew about that had been left on and was automatically sending out a signal they could pick up. It was possible, but again, it didn't seem very likely. They would have got to Bortsov a lot earlier if that had been the case.

He screwed his eyes up and did his best to clear them. Then he squinted even harder into the wind. He couldn't keep this up much longer. His eyes were watering so much now he could barely see. They would have to stop soon or they would be running off the road.

He just didn't know how the Russians had found Bortsov. He had no idea. But they had done it, clever bastards that they were, and he was angry and disgusted about the whole damn thing.

This job had been a heap of shit from the start. Last minute and improvised. No support. At minimum cost. Almost certainly off the books, too, from what Henderson had told him — and from what Henderson hadn't actually said. All in all, it looked even worse now than it had done at the start.

And this bloody car wasn't going much further either!

He cocked his head to listen to a new and even more urgent-sounding rattle, this one coming from the engine. He winced. He knew perfectly well what it was, and what it would take to fix it. It was a noise that demanded the attention of an experienced mechanic with a garage full of tools, equipment, skilled manpower, and a lot of spare parts.

* * *

'Have you got a passport?' Jake shouted over the shriek of the wind.

The passenger stuck his head up.

Jake repeated the question.

Bortsov nodded.

'Good.'

Jake wondered what name it would be in, not that it mattered much. One name was as good as another. Or as bad. The only significant question was whether or not the passport would stand up to scrutiny. Given that the guy was a career intelligence officer, Jake felt he was entitled to assume the answer was yes, and that the passport would withstand inspection at a not very busy border post.

The downside to that, of course, was that the people chasing Bortsov would know the name he was travelling under, unless he had had the foresight to equip himself with a second passport, one they didn't know about. That would be helpful, but there were no guarantees.

He shook his head, gave up and concentrated on driving. Some things were simply unknowable. What was it Donald Rumsfeld said that time, talking about issues facing the Bush administration in Washington? There were unknowns, the known unknowns, and then there were the unknown unknowns that nobody knew about!

That was it exactly. That was where he was himself right now. He knew next to nothing about any damn thing!

But other issues were more pressing now. For one, he was gradually freezing to death in the icy blast shrieking through the hole left by the disappeared windscreen. His face was stiff and he couldn't feel his hands any more. Could barely see either. He couldn't keep this up any longer. They were going to have to stop. Soon, very soon. And something was going to have to change.

CHAPTER FIFTEEN

The obvious route for them to take would have been along the coast and into Croatia just north-west of Herceg Novi, but Jake hadn't fancied that. It was too obvious, too direct. Too easy to anticipate. Besides, a little way past Tivat, they would have had to cross a sea inlet by a small ferry. An image of rats trapped in a cage with ferrets came to mind. He could do without that scenario.

So, his thinking had been to head north and take a roundabout route through Serbia. Now that, too, was up for reconsideration. The people chasing them knew which road out of Budva they had taken, and could well guess where they were headed now. It didn't seem sensible to continue as if nothing had happened. A change of route was needed.

First, though, they had to find another vehicle. This one was dying on them. If the noise before had been awful, the racket it was making now was horrendous, and he could feel the power draining away by the minute. Even with his foot hard down on the pedal, their speed was falling off.

Although Jake had to curse a lot, and hold his breath at times, the little Citroen kept going for another twenty minutes. It got them into Cetinje, a picturesque town in a hollow in the mountains, which at one time had been the capital of

Montenegro. On the edge of the town, he took his foot off the accelerator, moved the gear stick into neutral and coasted downhill, to avoid announcing their arrival with a terrifying cacophony of engine noise. With his foot hard on the brake, they swept down into the town and kept going until Jake spotted a place to park in a quiet, tree-lined street.

'Stay here,' he told Bortsov. 'I'm going to find another car.'

'Where are you—?'

Jake was too cold and overwrought to be bothered explaining himself further. It had been a rough couple of hours. 'Just stay here!' he snapped. 'I won't be long.'

* * *

Behind a big music pub that seemed to be the main attraction for the young people in Cetinje, he searched and found what he wanted: an old Skoda, a vehicle that conceivably was even older than the independent state of Montenegro. It was so decrepit that the owner hadn't bothered locking the doors. Jake's eyes gleamed as soon as he saw it. Exactly what he wanted!

Thank God there were still plenty of old bangers around in this country, he thought with relief. Modern cars, with all their electronics and computerised systems, were way beyond his capabilities to break into and get started.

He was inside and had the car hot-wired in a couple of minutes. The engine burst into life with a throaty roar. Wasting no time, he edged out of the parking lot and headed back to where he had parked the ruined hire car — and Bortsov.

'Come on!' he urged, rapping on his passenger's window.

'What . . . ?'

'Come on! Let's go.'

Bortsov stared for a moment and then reluctantly climbed out and allowed himself to be hurried into their new vehicle.

'This is not a good car,' he said with an audible sniff as soon as Jake was in the driver's seat.

'It'll do.'

Jake slammed his door shut and got them moving again. 'We're back in business,' he added, with something approaching satisfaction.

'It will do us no good,' Bortsov responded. 'In the end, they will find us.'

'You say that one more time,' Jake said, irritated almost beyond control, 'and I'll punch your miserable face in!'

CHAPTER SIXTEEN

'I am very tired,' Bortsov announced. 'I wish to rest now.'

'You can forget that, buddy!' Jake said with a snort of derision. 'We have miles to go before we sleep.'

'And there are promises I must keep,' his passenger said in a portentous voice, after a moment's pause. 'And miles and miles and miles to go before I sleep.' Jake was astonished, shocked even. He stared open-mouthed at Bortsov.

'Robert Frost,' Bortsov said with satisfaction. '"Stopping by Woods on a Snowy Evening". Published as part of his New Hampshire collection of 1923, but written in 1922.'

'Good God! You do surprise me. Do you know any more of it?'

'All of it,' Bortsov said complacently.

Jake chuckled. 'Oh, yeah! Of course you do.'

Bortsov recited the whole poem. Jake wasn't sure he had ever heard more than the couple of lines Ronald Reagan was supposed to have quoted in his inaugural presidential address, but what Bortsov said sounded right.

'All right, all right!' he snapped. 'That's enough.'

But damn, he thought. It was bloody impressive. Who would have thought it?

Then he chuckled. 'I didn't take you for a poetry enthusiast,' he said then in a more forgiving tone.

'Poetry enthusiast? No, I'm not.'

'You just happened to know that particular poem?'

'Yes.'

A little later, Jake said, 'Know any more poems by Robert Frost?'

'I know all of them.'

'All of them? There must be hundreds!'

'All of them,' Bortsov confirmed, sounding a bit bored by the subject.

Jake laughed. So the guy did have a sense of humour, after all!

He glanced sideways again, expecting to see an answering smile on Bortsov's face, but he didn't. No smile. Just the usual blank look. For a moment, he had the unsettling feeling that his passenger hadn't been joking.

CHAPTER SEVENTEEN

They headed next to Podgorica, Montenegro's modern capital. There, Jake left his passenger alone again while he went to obtain a better car legitimately. Surprisingly, the global car-hire company he found, admittedly a different one, let him have a VW Passat, a big — and very welcome — upgrade on the old Skoda he had stolen. Given what had happened to the last car he'd hired, he would gladly have taken anything they were prepared to offer — and wouldn't have been surprised if they had said: No — get lost!

So it was a fresh start. He felt now that they must have left the chasing pack far behind. They couldn't possibly have any idea where they were, but irritatingly, his passenger wasn't of the same opinion.

'They will know,' Bortsov said wearily. 'They know all. Everything.'

Frustrated, Jake wondered if he should just dump him and get the hell out. The guy was really getting on his nerves now with his infuriating and persistent defeatism. The negativity was wearing him down and making him wonder if there any point in persevering — he was meant to be doing the guy a favour! It wouldn't be long before his own interests might start to take precedence over moaning Bortsov's.

Then he reminded himself that the only reason he was here, doing this, was to protect Magda and their life together. If he could get rid of this miserable sod without it rebounding on Magda and himself, he would happily seize the opportunity, but at present there was no way of doing that. He was stuck for now.

One thing he knew for sure: he wasn't going to die for Bortsov, or for Henderson either. If it got really bad, he would bale out and take the consequences. His passenger might be important to Henderson, and possibly even to what might be thought of as the national interest, but Bortsov was a long way from being existentially important to Magda and himself.

Rehearsing all that in his head took the heat off and steadied Jake's temper. He got back to concentrating on the driving, and to plotting a route. He couldn't afford to let himself be distracted by petty irritants, such as an ungrateful, miserable, incurably sad apology for a human being like the man sitting next to him.

* * *

At Nikšić, he turned west again, having decided that Croatia and the coastal route might be a better bet after all. On reflection, Serbia's historical orientation towards Russia had made travelling through the country seem less attractive, especially considering where his passenger was from. Conversely, Croatia's traditional affinity with Western Europe was far more appealing.

Jake gave a wry smile and admitted to himself that he was doing little more than navigating by sticking a pin in the map. Instinct and intuition. Still, when logic and objectivity hit the buffers, you had to use what you had to hand. Nothing wrong with instinct and intuition then!

At Dolovi, they crossed the border into Bosnia and Herzegovina. A steep descent on a corkscrew road took them down past Trebinje and eventually close to the Croatian border near Dubrovnik.

They could have entered Croatia there, but then they would have had to leave it again, after a short distance, to pass through the twenty-kilometre beachhead on the coast that had been awarded to Bosnia in the Dayton Accord to prevent the country being entirely landlocked, before crossing the border into Croatia once more. The patchwork geography left over from the carving up of Yugoslavia all those years ago could really do your head in.

Instinct, again, told Jake to minimise their border crossings. They were bottlenecks and had always been dangerous places for people who were not innocent travellers. They were easy to keep under surveillance and they were where officialdom and bureaucracy tended to be at their peak, even at the best of times.

So they stayed on the Bosnian side of the border, on a road that paralleled the Croatian route along the coast. Finally — in darkness by then — they crossed into Croatia at Neum, at the northern end of Bosnia's twenty-kilometre strip of coast. Jake had anticipated a long delay there, but they were simply waved through with a surprising outbreak of minimal fuss and international cooperation. It was almost too easy, but he wasn't going to complain.

Their journey promised to be more straightforward after that. They were in well-developed Croatia, with a good, long run of a couple of hundred miles ahead of them to Trieste, and Italy. Jake began to breathe more easily.

'Hrvatska,' the passenger sniffed, breaking his long silence to use the Slavonic version of the name. 'It is not a good country, I think.'

'It will do me,' Jake assured him.

'A fascist country. It would have been better to go through Serbia. The Serbs welcome Russians. People like me,' he added.

'Oh, Russian, are you?' Jake said with a chuckle. 'Fancy that! I never knew.'

Bortsov shook his head in disgust at such childish comedy. 'They will find us here, anyway,' he said. 'I have seen the black car we saw near Budva. It has come for me.'

'Well, if they ask nicely, they can have you!' Jake assured him. 'Anyway, let me tell you something, my friend,' he added. 'The Balkan Wars are long over. And I'm one of those sensible people who have no wish to ever see them re-started by people like us. So we'll give Serbia a miss, thank you very much.'

'It will happen in any case,' his passenger said with a shrug, as he settled himself more comfortably in his seat. 'These wars are never over — not for long.'

You prejudiced, miserable old sod! Jake thought, not sure whether he was annoyed or amused. A bit of both, probably.

'You didn't really recognise that car, did you?' he asked as an afterthought.

'Yes. I saw the number plate.'

That shut Jake up.

CHAPTER EIGHTEEN

Despite Jake's hopes, Bortsov had it just about right. His pessimism was fully justified. The Balkan Wars didn't kick off again and they got through Croatia unscathed, but in Slovenia, on a main road, another attempt was made to ambush them. A powerful truck drew alongside and deliberately edged them towards the edge of the highway, where a drop down a steep hillside beckoned.

Bortsov yelped with alarm, but Jake had already assessed what was happening. He knew what to do. Without warning, he performed an emergency stop, standing on the brake. Bortsov slammed into the dashboard and Jake gritted his teeth and hung on to the steering wheel as the car shuddered and slithered to a smoking, screaming halt. The truck couldn't match deceleration like that, and carried on down the highway.

As soon as the truck was out of sight, Jake swung the car around and took off back the way they had come. A couple of miles down the road, he left the highway and resorted to a lattice of local roads until he felt it was safe enough to head on towards Italy via the autostrada.

Bortsov had said nothing after his first frightened scream, and Jake didn't encourage him to voice an opinion on what had happened. He had enough to do and to think about. But he did eventually concede to his passenger.

'You were right,' he said, when he had recovered and judged they were running safe. 'They do seem to know where we are.'

Bortsov nodded agreement. 'Always,' he said. 'They always do.'

'Well, that may have been true so far, but not anymore,' Jake said, irritated all over again. 'I don't want to hear another word about how bloody omnipotent your compatriots are!'

Bortsov shrugged, settled lower in his seat and sank back into silence.

* * *

Except, in Italy, just past Verona, it happened yet again. This time, a different tactic was employed. It was a classic box ambush, put in place without a hint of a warning. One car in front of them began to slow down. Another drew alongside, while a third closed up behind. All this in a matter of seconds. Ordinary, unconnected saloon cars suddenly coordinating and becoming a threatening strike force.

'What the hell?' Jake cried with anguish.

Desperate measures were called for yet again. He rammed the accelerator to the floor. The Passat took off, and Jake yanked the wheel hard, pushing the car up the hard shoulder to scrape past the block car in front.

Then it became a race, a high-speed chase that threatened to end in disaster. Bortsov screamed. Jake, heart pounding, clamped his teeth together. He changed down, stamped on the throttle and sent the rev counter all the way up into the red. The engine roared and whined. The little Passat shivered and shuddered, and leapt forward. Jake hung on to the steering wheel with one hand and used the other to change gear before the engine gave up and exploded.

He held the chasing cars at bay for a while, switching desperately between lanes, blocking their attempts to overtake him. But he couldn't keep it up. Once they operated as a team, with a car coming up on each side of him simultaneously, it would be over. There would be nowhere to go.

Seeing a turn-off approaching, he swung off the autostrada and hurtled into the centre of a town he'd never heard of. Desperate for attention from local cops, he tore through red lights at intersections and skidded across junctions and around corners, lights flashing and horn blaring. Bystanders, shoppers and onlookers dodged and ducked, jumped aside and ran for their lives.

But Jake couldn't lose the cars chasing them. One managed to clip their rear end as they slid round a corner. The Passat shuddered again, threatened to stall, but recovered. Jake changed down and pressed foot to floor.

Then, suddenly, his rear-view mirror was no longer full of vehicles trying to ram him off the road. The street behind was empty. He slowed down and down and down, suspicious as hell. Would they call it off just like that? Was this another ambush?

He circled around city blocks for minutes on end, eventually parking outside a big IT store on a modern retail park. Exactly what he needed.

'Keep your head down,' he snapped at Bortsov as he threw the door open and leapt out, heart still hammering like a piston gone wild.

There had been three cars in his mirrors. Two silver and one black, all of them unexceptional suburban saloons. Renaults, maybe. Or Insignia models. Fords, even. He could see none of them now.

But a police car raced past, followed by an ambulance. Both vehicles had their sirens and flashing lights going. He didn't need to ask what that was about.

'The black car crashed,' Bortsov said, answering the unasked question.

Jake ducked down to see him. 'What?'

'The black car. It crashed.'

'You're guessing?'

57

'I saw it.'

'What happened?'

'It couldn't get round a corner. It was going too fast, and hit a truck that was parked there.'

Jake got back inside and rested his forehead on the steering wheel for a moment, willing his pulse rate to fall to a sensible level.

'It was the same car,' Bortsov added.

'What do you mean?'

'The black car from Budva. It crashed.'

Jake nodded wearily. 'I suppose you're going to tell me you recognised the number plate again?'

'Yes.'

Jake just shook his head, his manic agitation starting to fade, the pounding in his chest slowing.

But Bortsov seemed calm enough, remarkably so. 'What now?' he asked.

'Have you got a phone?'

'Of course.'

'Give me it.'

'Why? Why should I . . . ?'

'Just give me the bloody phone!'

Bortsov hesitated a moment and then reached into his jacket pocket and pulled out a phone. He handed it over.

'What are you going to do with it?'

'Nothing. I just don't want you to do anything with it, either. Like making a phone call. I should have taken the bloody thing off you earlier.

'Now wait here for me — don't move!'

'What are you going to do? Steal another car?'

Jake shook his head. 'Not this time. I have something else in mind.'

* * *

One thing Jake knew for certain: he had to break the link. He had to stop them from knowing where they were. If he couldn't, they were heading for disaster. They would lead them all the way to Magda. He had to avoid that.

Then there was Bortsov to consider, another potential disaster. At the rate they were going, he would be lucky to keep him alive another day, never mind a whole bloody month.

He went inside the giant IT store and consulted a digital directory on one of the many screens in view. Then he headed for an escalator and the specialist technology section on the third floor. There, a thoughtful sales adviser listened to his requirements and in moments produced exactly what Jake wanted: an electronic bug detector. He paid cash for it and didn't bother waiting to hear advice about how to use it.

Back at the car, he ran the detector over the car. Nothing. Not a damned peep out of the bloody thing. Of course not. How could a bug have been attached to a random hire car?

He got back inside and slumped in his seat, feeling utterly defeated.

'They always win,' Bortsov said with apparent satisfaction. 'They are the best. You can't beat them.'

'Shut the fuck up!' Jake snapped.

Bortsov shrugged, turned his head and stared pointedly out of the window.

Jake switched on the engine, rammed the gear stick into first and got them moving again. If nothing else, they had to keep moving.

CHAPTER NINETEEN

Moscow

Oleg Blok knew some of what Bortsov could be taking to the West, but nowhere near all of it. Nobody else did either — it was impossible to know. The simple, cast-iron way of minimising the risk would be to eliminate him. One could only hope that the president's preference for a different course proved justified. Days gone by now and they were no nearer catching him. Kozlov though that too, judging by the look on his face.

'He got away,' the colonel said. 'We missed him.'

'What happened?'

Kozlov shrugged. 'He was in a hotel in Budva. But when the team arrived, he wasn't there. They waited, but he didn't return. He was gone. His possessions were abandoned in the hotel room.'

Blok raised his eyebrows. 'Everything was there?'

Kozlov shook his head. 'Nothing of value to us. Only personal stuff. Clothes. Toothbrush. That sort of thing.'

It sounded like their man had left in a hurry. Perhaps, Blok thought, he had been warned. He could even have been picked up by the Americans. Or else he had become uneasy and left of his own accord. Not that it mattered. What mattered was that he was gone.

'Do the team think he spotted them?'

Kozlov shook his head. 'They had only just arrived, and they went to his room as soon as they learned where it was. They say he couldn't have seen them.'

'Then perhaps the Americans have him?'

'It is possible, but unlikely. Who knows?' Kozlov added with a shrug. 'I wait to hear further.'

'If the Americans do have him, we must be careful. We don't want another incident.'

'Incident?'

'As in that village in the Tatra Mountains in Slovakia. The American contact team eliminated. We don't want the Americans thinking we're about to start World War Three.'

'An unfortunate accident. Don't worry, though. We will find him,' Kozlov said, clearly unhappy with the rebuke.

'Yes. And then I will decide what is to be done.'

Kozlov bit his tongue and said nothing more. He knew full well where the power lay in this investigation, and it was no longer with him even if he was head of department still.

He needed to be careful if he was to reassume control when Blok returned to his dacha, as was supposed to happen once this case was resolved. Kozlov knew perfectly well why Blok had been brought back: it was to do a specific job. Bortsov was his baby, as they said in Hollywood.

CHAPTER TWENTY

Jake, in the immortal British phrase from World War Two, kept calm and carried on. But they had been travelling now for many hours, and night was turning to day once again. Jake was tired and his passenger was comatose.

They kept going for a couple more hours. Then Jake gave in to exhaustion and stopped at a smart hotel beside a lake. They were offered a vacant suite, and Jake took it instantly. It was expensive, but Henderson was paying. At least, Jake hoped he would be, eventually. Extravagant, perhaps, but it was safer than he and Bortsov being in separate rooms on different floors, which was the alternative.

Room service was available twenty-four hours a day, but neither of them was interested in anything other than sleep. Despite everything that had happened, and knowing worse might lie ahead, Jake found sleep came easily.

* * *

After a late breakfast that could easily have been mistaken for lunch or even afternoon tea, given the time of day, they got moving again. A few hours of sleep had restored their spirits and improved the atmosphere between them. Something like normal conversation started to occur, despite Bortsov seeming to be a taciturn man by nature.

Jake was feeling more charitable after his night's rest. His companion had been travelling a hard road for some time, and Jake knew from experience how that could wear down even the strongest eventually.

'How long had it been since you last slept?' he asked.

'I don't remember.' Bortsov shrugged. 'Many days. I need to rest more. My brain is not working properly.'

'I understand. You've had a tough time.'

Bortsov glanced at him speculatively. 'Perhaps you know what it is like?'

Jake shook his head. 'I doubt it. Not exactly, anyway.'

'No, perhaps not,' Bortsov said, nodding. 'How could you? Even I did not.'

* * *

Back on the road, and thinking about the difficulties they had encountered, Jake realised there was a pattern, or a constant factor, that he hadn't noticed until now. If the people chasing Bortsov wanted to kill him, he would surely already be dead. Himself, too, probably. There had been enough opportunities to blast away with machineguns instead of trying to . . . Trying to do what? Force them off the road? Recapture Bortsov?

He frowned. Abduction rather than assassination? Could that be the plan? Impossible to know, but what Jake did know was that killing Bortsov would have been easier to arrange than what had actually happened. The more he thought about it, the more he believed they really did want him alive.

Well, he thought with a wry smile, that possibility was something to cling to, even if the Russians were unlikely to feel the same way about himself. To them, he would just be fluff, and then collateral damage.

* * *

After a couple of hours, he pulled into a service area. Coffee would be good. And it was time to phone Magda. There were things he needed to tell her. A change of plan was one of them. While the passenger was away looking for the toilets, Jake made the call and began to explain how things stood.

'I'm not going to take him straight there now, as we planned. They've been on our backs the whole damned way and I don't want to risk leading them to our front door. It's uncanny how they seem to know exactly where we are, and where we're going.'

'A leak, perhaps?'

'I don't see how it could be. Nobody was told where we were going, and I didn't even have a route in mind myself.'

'A tail, then?'

'Possibly. But I haven't seen any signs of one. Every now and again, they just turn up — right on top of us. I wondered if they were somehow tracking us, but . . .' He paused and shook his head. 'Anyway, we've survived so far.

'Another odd thing about it, though, is that I'm not sure now that they actually want to kill him. They won't be bothered about me, of course, but I think they may want to abduct him, rather than kill him.'

'Why do you say that? Are you sure?'

'I'm not sure about any damn thing! But it's the only explanation that makes sense. Several times, they could have just shot the hell out of us, if that was what they wanted to do. But they didn't even try. So I've begun to think it's abduction rather than assassination they're here for. Perhaps he's still valuable to them, as well as to Henderson.'

Magda thought for a moment and then said, 'They could want to find out what he knows, and who has helped him, before they kill him. I'm afraid it will be painful for him, if that is the case.'

'Yes,' Jake said with a wince. He knew exactly what she meant. It wouldn't be an easy death, and it was inconceivable that they would allow him to live once the interrogation was over.

'So, if you don't want to risk leading them here, what are you thinking of doing?'

'I want to take him somewhere more remote, and more defensible. Keeping him out of harm's way for a whole month is feeling like a bigger challenge now than I thought it would be.'

'Where, then? Any ideas?'

'Yes, actually. I won't say the name of the place I have in mind, just in case the line's tapped, but I was thinking of where we went last summer. Remember?'

She laughed. 'How could I forget?'

He smiled, his own memory also refreshed. They had had a wonderful time last summer.

'So what do you think?'

'That might be better,' Magda said thoughtfully. 'Yes. I agree with you. A good idea! I will find somewhere there for us to stay.'

'Good. Thank you. I must go now,' he added, seeing Bortsov on his way back to the car. 'Take care, sweetheart. Stay safe.'

'You, too, darling!'

CHAPTER TWENTY-ONE

Moscow

Blok had to acknowledge that Kozlov's team had done a good job tracking Bortsov to Budva. They shouldn't have lost him in the first place, of course — he should have been intercepted back in Slovakia, if not sooner. But given that hadn't happened, they had recovered well.

Much as he hated admitting it, Bortsov had done well, too. Either that or he had just been plain lucky. He had evaded the original ambush that had taken out the American extraction team. Then he had somehow got himself to Montenegro. That wouldn't have been easy, given that he didn't seem to have had help at that stage. One had to wonder how he had managed it.

Even more interesting was the question of why he had gone to Montenegro, and to Budva, in particular. That wasn't an escape route he would have expected a man in Bortsov's position to take, or even to know about. Was it a country, and a place, that he knew, and where he felt safe? That was doubtful. Or had he been instructed to go there? That was the explanation that made most sense.

It was still an odd choice, whoever had made it. Montenegro wasn't a country of interest to the Americans. It was very small, thinly populated and generally of no account. Also, for them, the Americans, it was not really a friendly country. Traditionally, its people leaned towards Russia, whatever the current government might say and think about NATO and the EU.

Still, for whatever reason, it must have been the Americans who had steered him there. They would have enticed him and made the offer that had persuaded him to run. So, it would have been them who had told him where to go. It was unlikely that anyone else had the interest, and no one else could offer as much as they could to a potential defector.

Blok stared at the wall map of Western Europe he had had installed. The obvious reason to make for Budva would have been if Bortsov expected, or hoped, to be extradited by sea. That wasn't the usual American way, though, certainly not in Europe. No, he would have expected them to take their man west and north, through the Czech Republic or Poland, perhaps to one of the big American bases in Germany. From there, it would have been possible to fly him anywhere in the world unobserved and without hindrance. But that hadn't happened. He shook his head and sighed. There was something more complex afoot, he was sure.

* * *

Blok was still staring at the map when Kozlov returned.

'He's in Italy now.'

'Italy?'

'He ran through Croatia, along the coast, and into Italy. Now he's . . .'

'He is being followed?'

'At a distance. They have made two attempts to stop him but were unsuccessful.'

Blok looked askance. 'Unsuccessful?'

'He could have been eliminated, but your orders were to take him alive.' Kozlov shrugged. 'I understand why, of course, but that is more difficult to accomplish.'

Blok clenched his fists. Why difficult? It wouldn't have been in his day. What sort of operation were these fools running? Perhaps it was just that he hadn't yet gained full control. Kozlov wouldn't openly obstruct him, but a lack of enthusiasm could amount to the same thing.

'Tell me, Boris,' he said slowly, 'how is it that you know so well where Bortsov is?'

'We do it the old way, General. Remember that?'

It took a moment before Blok fully appreciated what was being said.

'Really?'

Kozlov nodded.

Blok smiled. Something, at last, to be pleased about.

'Well done, Boris,' he said quietly. 'The old ways are often the best, even now. So we know exactly where he is — but not where he is going?'

'Very true.' Kozlov frowned. 'There is something else we need to consider. He has help. He couldn't have got this far alone.'

'The Americans, presumably,' Blok said.

'We believed we had got rid of them in Slovakia.'

'They must have provided backup, a secondary protection team.'

'Perhaps.'

Blok thought about it some more, wondering if the president really was right to want Bortsov captured rather than just eliminated. As Kozlov had said, killing him would be a lot easier. They knew where he was. They could get rid of him whenever they chose and bring the whole sorry business to an end.

Well, it might come to that, he thought, but not yet.

'Tell your men to back off, Boris. Continue to follow him, but no more attacks until further notice.'

Kozlov raised his eyebrows.

'Let's at least see where he is going, and with whom.'

'It's a risk,' Kozlov pointed out with a frown.

'One worth taking. As the president himself said, we need to know more about how this defection was organised. Bortsov himself won't have all the answers, clever as he is.'

* * *

Later, Blok pored again over the list he had made of information Bortsov might have taken. He knew it was only a fraction of what he could disclose, given the special nature of the man. Yet he had to try to assess the damage that would result if it got to the Americans.

He winced when he looked at the list of sleepers in the US, the agents who had been planted there and were living ordinary American lives until such time as they might be called on to actually do something. They were important. He knew that only too well. Such a resource was inestimable. On the other hand, they were also expendable. If the worst came to the worst, they could be sacrificed and given heroes' memorials. Russia was good at that — and Russia would still exist.

Then there was the portfolio of investments, intended to give financial returns when the oil and gas prices slumped, as well as influence and technical information. All important, but critical? Scarcely. Nothing to risk starting a war over.

The blueprint for using soft power to cause chaos in a country in the old Soviet sphere of interest was much more troublesome. In the wrong hands, that could cause serious difficulties. Again, though, Russia would survive intact.

Enough! Wearily, he pushed the pile of documents aside. 'Boris!' he called. 'We need to talk.'

CHAPTER TWENTY-TWO

'I suppose you are CIA?' Bortsov said just after they had crossed into France.

Jake looked askance at him, and then smiled and chortled. 'CIA? Whatever gave you that idea?'

'What else could you be?'

Jake shook his head. 'Anything! But the CIA is what you expected?'

'Them or the FBI.'

'The FSB, you mean, don't you?' Jake said, chuckling still.

'FSB?' Bortsov shook his head. 'They will not help me.'

'Because you sold out to Uncle Sam?'

'Who?'

'The Americans.'

Bortsov didn't answer for a moment. Jake had the feeling their conversation had been derailed. Neither of them seemed to have a firm hold on it. Jake even wondered if Bortsov really knew who he was defecting to. Perhaps it had all been a spur-of-the-moment thing.

'The FSB are afraid of the GRU,' Bortsov said eventually. 'That is why they would not help me, even if I asked.'

Jake shook his head again at the intricacies of the world of Russian Intelligence. They're worse than our lot, he decided.

Still, he'd learned something, or had it confirmed: Bortsov was — or had been — GRU. The FSB probably had every right to be scared of helping someone like him. They were military and killers. Assassins and poisoners. A thoroughly nasty bunch who knew no boundaries. Friend and foe alike feared them.

So that was who they were up against.

'I've got news for you, pal,' Jake said, trying to get things back on track. 'I am not American.'

'Maybe, maybe not. But you still work for them.'

Jake was beginning to despair. This conversation was getting surreal. What on earth was in the man's head?

'I never have, and I don't believe I ever will work for or with the CIA,' he said firmly.

Plainly, Bortsov didn't believe a word of it. Perhaps, Jake thought, he just didn't believe anything at all that anyone ever said to him anymore. Hardly surprising. Experience had taught him to be disappointed. And now confusion was rife in his unhappy world.

'Why do any of them want you, anyway?' Jake asked. 'What have you done? What have you got, or know?'

'That doesn't matter.'

'To me, it does.'

'Well, you can go to hell!' Bortsov said, suddenly sounding angry.

'Nice.' Jake nodded, slightly taken aback at the first show of emotion from the Russian the entire trip. 'I go to all the trouble of rescuing you, and that's the thanks I get?'

'If it hadn't been for you Americans, I wouldn't have been in this position. I would have been continuing with my life, instead of trying to follow my dream.'

'I told you,' Jake said doggedly, 'I've got nothing to do with the Americans. Anyway,' he added, 'it can't all be down to them that you're in this situation. You've played a part too.'

No response.

'I suppose the coup failed, didn't it? Is that why you're in trouble? The Montenegro government survived, and the country became a NATO member. So it's all your fault?'

Bortsov stared at Jake as if he were deranged.

'What?' Jake said defensively.

'Such rubbish you talk! I am surprised they sent someone as stupid as you.'

Jake grinned. 'Thank you very much! Which part is rubbish? Are you going to tell me you had nothing to do with the attempted coup?'

'In Montenegro? Of course not.'

The tone was contemptuous and dismissive. Bortsov looked around and stared out of the window at the unfamiliar landscape for a moment before adding, 'I want some coffee.'

'Soon. We'll stop soon. What did you mean—?'

Bortsov gave a weary sigh. 'Is that what you believe? It is about something that happened in Podgorica?'

'That's what I was told, yes.'

The other man gave a cynical laugh and shook his head. 'You know nothing, in that case. You, too, have been fooled.'

Jake was stung into silence. Was the guy play-acting or speaking the truth? If the latter, he might have to recalibrate and think things over. Had Henderson been economical with the truth, or even lying, for example?

'What about you?' Bortsov asked suddenly. 'Why are you here? Why did you agree to come?'

It was a fair question. Why not tell him? Jake thought. After all, if they were to survive the next month, they needed to be more trusting of each other.

'Because I'm trapped, Yuri — just like you seem to be.'

There was a small hiatus in the conversation then, as if they each needed to take note of the fact that Jake had used Bortsov's given name for the first time.

'My name is Jake, by the way.'

'Jake?'

'Jake Ord.'

Bortsov nodded, seemingly appreciative that such information had been imparted.

'I am Yuri Bortsov, as you seem to know. At least, I used to be before . . .' He paused. 'Trapped? Why are you trapped?'

'I'm British,' Jake said. 'The woman I live with — who will join us eventually, by the way — is an illegal immigrant in the UK. To make it worse, she has a criminal record in her own country. The British authorities know that, and could deport her if they wished.'

'Ah!' Bortsov nodded with understanding. 'So they have blackmailed you?'

'Exactly.'

'What will they do if you don't help them?'

Jake shrugged. 'I'm not sure. Expel her and charge me with helping and concealing her, probably. But I don't really know. Maybe nothing at all. But I can't take the risk of our lives being totally disrupted.'

'Of course.' Bortsov nodded again, this time emphatically. 'It is the same in my country. Many things are possible, if you don't do what they want you to do.'

CHAPTER TWENTY-THREE

Southern Portugal

Nothing happened in France or in Spain, except they drove
— on and on. Jake got in the groove and kept going on
automatic. He and Magda had travelled this route the year
before. So he knew where he was going. All he had to do was
keep going until they got there. He was focused.

Yuri, too, was focused. Mostly he slept, as if in hiberna-
tion. Jake was OK with that. It made things simpler for him.
Less to be agitated about.

Then at last they were there, in southern Portugal, the
Algarve. They boarded the ferry from Olhão at the very last
minute, just as the crew were about to remove the gangway.
A few minutes later, Magda, from her vantage point on the
ship, phoned to confirm that no one had boarded after them.

Jake ended the call and nodded to Bortsov with satisfaction. 'It looks like we're OK.'

'Perhaps,' Bortsov responded, clearly unable — or unwilling — to believe it.

Together with another fifty or so people, they found
seats on the hard wooden benches of the *Mira Sado*. Looking
around, Jake could see no obvious threat amongst their

fellow passengers. Mostly, they were elderly. A mixture of tourists come to stay or to visit for the day and residents and workers returning from the mainland with their laden shopping bags. There were a few children amongst them, some travelling alone. So far as he could see, there were no young male adults, which was reassuring.

A young girl with her small pet dog in a plastic carry-cage beside her caught his eye and smiled. He reciprocated, and for the first time in several days felt like a human being again. Careful! he warned himself. He couldn't afford to let his guard down.

At least Bortsov was behaving. Sitting there calmly, looking around occasionally, he seemed more interested in what was going on than he had at any point in their long journey. Perhaps fear and fatigue had receded a little, or had been overcome by the prospect that he might just escape his hunters. Perhaps he, too, was beginning to feel human again.

Jake felt a surge of compassion. The man had been through a lot. Time on the island, where they were going, would do him good. Even so, he couldn't wait to get rid of him. Only three weeks to go now until that happened. Already he had used up a whole week of the time he had committed to Henderson. Correction: three weeks and a bit to go. Then he and Magda would be free to get on with their lives.

As the shore receded and the ferry entered more open water, a strong and chilling breeze began to sweep over the open benches where they were sitting. It soon made things uncomfortable and conversation difficult. Jake got to his feet and suggested that, as others were doing, they should move into the shelter of the big cabin.

'We're going to the island of Armona,' he said as they sat down inside. 'There hasn't been any time for us to talk about it, but that's where we're headed.'

'Armona?' the passenger said in a wondering tone. 'What country is that?'

'Portugal still. Armona is a small island off the southern coast, one among many. The whole area,' Jake added, sweeping his arm around to encompass all they could see, and more, 'is part of the Ria Formosa National Park. The plan is for us to stay there for the next couple of weeks. My partner and I will look after you while longer-term arrangements for you are made by people in London. You should be perfectly safe. Just think of it as a holiday — and relax!'

'A holiday?' Bortsov said incredulously. 'Relax? At a time like this?'

'It's what I've been asked to do,' Jake said with a shrug. 'Look after you for another three weeks. To me, now we're here, it's a holiday. You can call it whatever you like.'

* * *

They left the ferry and set off along the timber jetty leading to the sandy shore. As previously agreed, Magda had kept her distance during the journey in order to keep an eye out for anyone watching them. Jake hadn't even seen her. But now he spotted her, tall and slender, stern faced, already onshore and waiting outside the bar-cum-café that was the largest building at the terminus. He nudged Bortsov, and they shuffled steadily forward amid the torrent of fellow passengers heading for land.

'Welcome to Armona!' Magda said with a smile that lit up her face when they reached her.

Bortsov shook her hand but was unimpressed. 'Armona,' he repeated, looking around with a disparaging glance. 'It isn't much, I think.'

Magda gave him another smile, a thinner one this time. Already, Jake felt, she was just as unimpressed with Bortsov as the man himself was with Armona.

'It's good enough for us, Yuri. Paradise, I should think, compared with where you've come from.' Jake patted his reluctant companion on the shoulder.

'Humph,' Bortsov said.

Jake turned to Magda. 'Right, lead the way, my dear.'

She turned and motioned for them to follow her as she set off walking. Bortsov looked inclined to protest about that, as well, but somehow managed to contain himself. He must have expected a limo, Jake thought with a smile.

* * *

Ungracious thought his comment about Armona had been, Bortsov had it about right. In truth, it really wasn't very much at all. But Jake didn't care. He and Magda had enjoyed their holiday here, and he was happy to return. He just hoped the island would prove a safe refuge for them for the time that was left of their month-long babysitting contract with Henderson.

It wasn't a very big island. To say it was three miles long and half a mile wide would be to seriously misrepresent things, exaggerate the island's size even. Much of its length consisted of a low-lying expanse of gleaming white sand. Although not actually inaccessible, the absence of any paths and the difficulty of trudging through the exceptionally soft sand were, if not a physical barrier, certainly a big constraint in the heat. The inhabited and visited part of the island was a postage-stamp-sized beach resort at the south-west corner, where the ferry had landed.

From the ferry terminal, the island's only paved walkway spanned the length of the settlement, with cabins, chalets, shacks and small cottages double-banked to either side. It was along that pedestrian walkway, perhaps half a mile in length, that Magda led them now. They were accompanied by everyone else who had disembarked from the ferry, people gradually dropping off as they reached their destination.

'It is a poor place, I think,' Bortsov commented after a few minutes.

'But safe,' Jake told him sharply.

'You think so?'

'I do.'

'Perhaps.'

Magda smiled. 'Just think of your stay here as a holiday,' she suggested brightly, much as Jake had done earlier.

'A holiday?' Bortsov shook his head. 'Most of these dachas are very poor — substandard, I think. It is not like Krima. That, I like very much for a holiday. Krima is truly beautiful.'

'Krima?' Jake said.

'Crimea,' Magda interpreted. 'It's the Russian name for it. And Yuri is right. It is very beautiful there. That's why the tsars and most of the other European royal families used to spend summers in Crimea.'

'Exactly!' Bortsov said. 'You have been there?'

'I have.'

'Oh,' Jake contributed, wondering if it was the same now Putin owned it. But he wasn't really interested. He just felt like telling Bortsov to shut up.

However, he didn't. It was hot and they were both tired. Magda too, probably. He didn't underestimate the pressure she was under.

All he really wanted right now was for Bortsov to keep walking. There was no powered transport here, and he wasn't going to carry him. As long as the man kept walking, he could think and say what he liked. For the moment, at least. Within reason.

At the same time, he had to acknowledge that, in a way, Bortsov was right about Armona. This wasn't a ritzy five-star resort of the sort visited by international celebs, never mind royalty. It was more of a cheerful working-class retirement home-cum-weekend resort.

A few dwellings looked new, and were well designed and built, but a lot were old and shabby DIY creations. The latter were the product of freelance private enterprise and initiative, built over generations by an army of individuals armed with little more than their own resources, time, ingenuity and a lot of loving commitment.

And there were the astonishing gardens in front of the cottages. Jake had to smile as he recalled their amazement when he and Magda had first come here. They were gardens the like of which he wouldn't have believed existed without seeing them for himself.

For a start, there was no soil on the island. Everything that was growing here grew in sand, the pure, white sand of which the island consisted. And it was very hot and dry for much of the year. Yet things still grew, often wonderfully well. Most of the cottages had beautiful little gardens, swamped by massed flowering plants and shrubs. There were trees, too: pines and tamarisks, eucalyptus and shady, broad-leafed evergreens that he couldn't identify. Somehow their roots reached down and found the water and nutrients they needed, just as they did, Jake supposed, in a Saharan oasis.

Magda turned off the main walkway. They followed her, threading between a few dilapidated shacks and abandoned cottages until they came to a building rather larger than most, and in decidedly better condition.

'We are here,' she announced.

She advanced confidently, almost proudly, along the short path to unlock the front door and throw it wide open. With a smile, she stood aside. Bortsov hesitated — for a moment, Jake feared he would refuse to enter. Then he shook his head and stepped forward, acquiescing but making clear this was not what he had anticipated when he made his bold run to the West.

'Too bad, mate,' Jake said cheerfully. 'You should have read the small print before you signed on.'

'What?'

'*Caveat emptor*, old cock! Buyer beware.'

Bortsov looked outraged for a moment, suspecting, rightly, an insult, if one that was incomprehensible to him. Then his shoulders slumped in defeat and he made his way inside.

That's better, Jake thought, amused. We don't need any more tantrums. Our time together is going to be difficult enough without more of that.

CHAPTER TWENTY-FOUR

The cottage was small, but it was in decent condition and more than adequate for their needs. There were two bedrooms, and a kitchen, bathroom and big living room. That was it, apart from the large terrace or balcony at the back, from where they could look out across sand flats and an inlet of the sea to the mainland.

Bortsov continued to give the impression that he would rather be elsewhere, probably anywhere but where he actually was. He had withdrawn into himself again, having delivered his view of the island and its quality — or lack of it. Exhaustion, probably, Jake decided. The cottage itself met with neither open approval nor disgust from Mr Bortsov. For the moment, it seemed, he had exhausted his store of critical comments. However, he did appear relieved to be able to sit down somewhere quiet at last, somewhere that wasn't a fast-moving vehicle, and he made no complaints about the bedroom he had been allocated or the fact that he had no clothes with him but those he was wearing, which were now badly in need of a wash. Exhaustion had its compensations, Jake decided. It was something of a blessing so far as he was concerned. He had just about had enough of him. Compassion had its limits.

'Yuri has nothing in the way of clothes,' he told Magda, 'and I don't have much more myself. We had to drop everything in Budva and run, leaving all his stuff behind. I was lucky to get him out.'

'Well, I have brought a few things for you both. Shirts, socks and underwear.' Magda paused, looking thoughtful, and then added, 'We can check to see what else you need. If we can't get clothing on the island, I'll make a shopping trip to Olhão.'

'The mainland?' Jake grimaced. 'I'm not so sure about that.'

'The Russians don't know about me,' Magda pointed out. 'It will be safe.'

Jake nodded, reluctantly accepting the point. She was probably right. They couldn't possibly know about her.

'OK. If it's necessary.'

'First, though, would you like a beer?'

'Excellent idea!'

Magda produced a couple of bottles from the fridge and got Jake to find glasses in a kitchen cupboard. Bortsov happily accepted the glass of beer Jake handed him, and even thanked him for it. Then they all toasted one another, Jake saying that for now their travelling was done.

'Perhaps,' Bortsov said, reserving his position.

Jake smiled. He was feeling more relaxed now he had a beer in hand, and he was ready to allow his charge more leeway. The negativity was not going to get to him anymore, he told himself. Another three weeks with this miserable bastard was going to be a tough sentence, but he could take it now he had Magda along to share it with him.

From his seat on one of the two sofas, he nursed his beer and idly watched as Magda picked up and examined the bug detector he had bought to use on the car. He told her what it was.

'The car was clean,' he concluded. 'So it was a waste of money.' After a moment's reflection, he added, 'I'll have to decide what to do about the car. I could get the hire company to come to Olhão to pick it up, but it might be better just to leave it there for now. We might need it again.'

Magda nodded. She was abstracted, still examining the bug detector.

'I assume you came by car?' Jake said.

'Truck,' she said absently. 'I brought your old truck.'

That made sense, Jake thought. So they might not need the hire car anymore after all.

Magda continued fiddling with the bug detector. She pressed a button, and it immediately started beeping. They looked at each other with astonishment, and then in Jake's case with consternation.

'What the hell?' He leapt to his feet.

Magda got up and walked across the room to run the device over the plastic bags he and Bortsov had accumulated on their journey. She got nothing there. It was the same when she tested the jackets they had tossed aside. No signal.

'And me and my possessions,' Magda said thoughtfully, with a glance at her own things, 'they don't even know about.'

'Yet,' Jake pointed out.

'Yes, yet.'

Bortsov got up and eased past Magda on his way to look out of the window. The gadget immediately started going wild.

'It's him!' Magda gasped.

Jake swore again and spun round.

Bortsov turned, too, and glared at them both. 'What?' he demanded. 'What have I done now?'

'It's you setting this thing off,' Jake said, struggling to stay calm. 'Somehow. So now we know.'

'Know what?'

'How they did it. How they knew where we were all the time.'

Bortsov glanced from one to the other of them, and then at the gadget in Magda's hand. She raised it and pointed it at him, moving up close as she did so. Immediately, the beeping re-commenced.

He paled and looked devastated. His eyes darted desperately around the room, as if he were looking for an escape route.

'Did you know about this?' Jake demanded.

Bortsov shook his head. 'No, not exactly.'

The qualification made it an incriminating admission.

'You knew,' Jake said flatly. 'And said nothing, you bastard!'

Bortsov shook his head, but added, 'I didn't know, but I suspected . . . something.'

'Something like this?'

He shrugged, looking glum. 'Something.'

'Empty your pockets.'

Bortsov did as he was told. Out came . . . very little. Tissues, keys, glasses in a case, Russian passport, pen, loose change — coins of various currencies and denominations — and a wallet. Jake dumped everything on a little table and had Bortsov step back. Magda ran the gadget over the small pile. Nothing. No beeping at all.

Jake swore and glared at Bortsov. 'Now your clothes. Get them off!'

They were past the point where Bortsov could have refused. Jake had a full head of steam behind him now. The Russian shrugged and disrobed.

The heap of clothing didn't set the beeper off again. Nothing happened. Magda pointed the detector at Bortsov himself, and that did it. Once again, the beeping filled the room.

Grim-faced, Jake told him to get dressed again and turned away, defeated.

'You said you suspected . . . something?' Magda said.

Bortsov nodded. 'In my bones, perhaps. Something like that.'

'In your bones?' Jake said, catching on. 'What the hell do you mean by that?'

'Something,' Bortsov repeated with another shrug.

'That's why you kept saying we'd never get away from them?'

'If I had told you, you would not have helped me,' Bortsov said, defiant now.

'You're right there, my friend,' Jake said, feeling both frustrated and angry.

Bortsov said nothing more. He just hung his head. The defiance had leached away. He looked ready to collapse.

Jake turned away to hide his anger. He stared out of the window without seeing anything of the view, his brain doing somersaults as it wrestled with this new development.

What the hell was it? What had they done to him? An injection of Strontium 90 in his bones? Or what?

Then there was the old question of why. What did they want from him? Why was he so damned important to them that they couldn't bear the thought of losing him? Why mark him like this?

'Jake?' Magda said quietly.

'What?'

'Go easy on him.'

He gave a little snort of derision.

'It's not his fault.'

That, at least, was true, Jake had to admit. Whatever it was, he hadn't done it to himself. But he hadn't helped himself either. He could at least have suggested how they might be being tracked. Instead he'd said nothing at all, and it could have cost them both their lives. It still might. Magda's, as well, now.

Yet, if he had said something, what would have happened then? Bortsov's fear, obviously, had been that he would be abandoned and left to cope alone. His fear was fully justified. That might very well have happened. Jake knew he would probably have told Henderson he was baling out, in that case — and to hell with the consequences. Christ, what a mess! he thought, rubbing his face with his hands.

'I think I know the answer, Jake. What we must do.'

It took a moment for Magda's comment to register. When it did, he turned round to stare at her.

'So tell me,' he demanded.

CHAPTER TWENTY-FIVE

'So tell me,' Jake repeated.

'I think they may have put a pellet in him, underneath his skin. The old KGB used to do that. The modern FSB, GRU or wherever he comes from quite possibly still do.'

'A pellet? What, like a homing beacon, a tracker?'

'Yes. It is possible, I think.'

'Like we microchip dogs?'

'Exactly.'

Jake shook his head. How the hell did she know stuff like this? Not for the first time, her former involvement with the Prague criminal world was proving useful. Prague was a city full of active and renegade spies, and people moving in certain circles would know a lot about them and how they worked — e.g. Magda!

She stepped up close to Bortsov and switched the gadget on again, with the same result. She moved it around him. The beeping varied slightly, the variations clearly discernible.

'It's somewhere in his back,' Magda concluded. 'Low down.'

Jake nodded as he mulled it over. Magda's suggestion was still just that, a possibility, but it was plausible, and it gave him a ray of hope. It might be the explanation of how the Russians had been able to follow them across Europe. How he had needed that!

'What do you think? Would they do something like that?' he asked Bortsov, who had been a bystander during this investigatory process. 'Something in your back, but under the skin, not in your bones?'

Bortsov shrugged. 'It is possible, yes.'

'Any idea where it could be?'

'No, but the monitor will tell us exactly.'

Jake was astonished. A helpful suggestion? And Yuri saying 'us' so positively? Good God! Was he onside at last?

'OK,' he said, nodding. 'Let's try it.'

They soon identified the hotspot, the place where the monitor went mad. It was in his backside. Of course it was. That was where it had to be, wasn't it? Jake thought grimly. Maximum discomfort to remind you of them at all times.

Bortsov undid his belt, pulled his trousers down and turned round. And there it was! A red indentation in his backside from a freshly healed wound. It looked as if Magda was right. This was how it had been done.

Jake sighed and shook his head. 'They knock you out at any time recently?' he asked. 'Anaesthetise you during a medical examination, perhaps?'

'We have medical examinations all the time. They do things to you without explaining them. You can't ask.'

'Well, we might have to do that again. We've got to get this thing out of you.'

* * *

Jake called a time out and asked Bortsov to help Magda make a pot of tea. While they were doing that, he went out on to the balcony and called Henderson for the first time since the start of the operation, using the burner phone he had been given.

'No names,' he said initially, 'and I'll keep it brief. We have your man. So far, we've managed to ward off the opposition and survive. The problem is they keep on catching up with us, again and again, and we've only just figured out how they're doing it. It seems they've microchipped him.'

'Good heavens! That old Soviet trick?'

'Yeah. So I'm told.'

'A tracker, eh? Sometimes that was also how they used to smuggle information across borders and between countries. Other times they just used microdots.'

'I didn't know that.'

Jake shook his head and listened for a few moments before breaking in again. 'Well, what I really want to know is how deep the chip will be? Any idea?'

'It won't be deep at all. Subcutaneous, I should think. Just under the surface.'

'Thanks. That's all I need to know.'

'What are you thinking of doing?'

'Getting it out. Nothing more at the moment.'

Jake ended the call. He stood gazing into the misty distance for a moment and wondered how brave Bortsov was. Possibly very, given his career trajectory, and how far he had come since abandoning it. He had certainly needed to have been tougher than he'd appeared so far, anyway.

At least they had time to do what needed to be done. A couple of hours, at the very least. Nothing else was going to happen before the next ferry arrived the next morning.

CHAPTER TWENTY-SIX

They plied Bortsov with strong drink, fed him paraceta-mol and did their level best to distract him from what was to come. When the time arrived for the talking to stop, he unbuckled his belt once again, laid face down on the bed and urged them to get on with it.

Jake steeled himself for the task ahead. He took the sharp kitchen knife Magda had sterilised in boiling water and began to dig, peeling back a layer of skin from the small area where the wound was. The pellet took some digging out, but not as much as the fragments of bullets he had dug out of himself and others in a past life. As ever, he reminded himself that needs must. To Bortsov's credit, and to Jake's relief and surprise, the patient made not a sound during the process.

When the pellet came out, Magda handed over a ster-ile swab she had taken from a first aid kit in the cottage. Jake cleaned the wound, put in a couple of stitches and then applied a dressing.

'It's over,' he said with relief, stepping back. 'Job done.'
'Well done, Doctor!' Magda said.
'All in a day's work,' Jake grinned, affecting nonchalance.
'I'm impressed.'

'I've had a hard life. Learned some useful things along the way.'

Bortsov gave him a nod of appreciation when he gingerly turned over on to his side. 'Thank you,' he said, which was another surprise.

'You'll have to be careful,' Jake told him. 'Where they put the chip wasn't exactly intended for your comfort or convenience.'

'It is what they do,' Bortsov said with a shrug. 'It is to remind you of them.'

Jake thought that sounded about right and was amused that he'd had the same thought himself.

He rinsed the pellet in a bowl of water, held it out for Bortsov to see and then dropped it on the floor and made to crush it beneath his heel.

'Don't destroy it!' Bortsov said urgently.

Jake stared at him, foot hovering.

'We may still need it.'

'How much?'

'I don't know. A lot, possibly.'

'Then that gives us a problem. We need to stop it sending out the signal.'

'Yes,' Bortsov said.

'Let me think about it.'

'Not for long,' Magda warned.

* * *

While Jake did some thinking, Magda gave their patient a couple of extra pills — stronger painkillers this time — and tucked him up in bed. He was pretty woozy by then, which Jake didn't find surprising. The guy had been through a lot before now, and what had just happened hadn't been much fun.

'What do you think?' he asked Magda when she'd seen Bortsov to bed.

'About what?'

'Him, for starters.'

She shrugged. 'He should sleep now. And we've done our best to keep infection at bay. Let's just wait and see what he's like tomorrow.'

'Tomorrow? He isn't going to sleep that long, surely?'

'At least until tomorrow,' she said, 'considering the medication I've given him.'

Looking askance, Jake said, 'I hope you know what you're doing?'

'So do I,' she said with a grin.

He chuckled and then turned serious again. 'What can we do about the pellet? Any ideas?'

'It seems we may need to keep it.'

'Yes. Perhaps there's information on it that he doesn't want to lose. His passport to a new life in the West, maybe. Henderson said the KGB used to send information across borders that way sometimes. But we have to stop it functioning as a homing beacon. That's my priority.'

Magda frowned for a moment. Then she said, 'Freeze it.'

'Freeze it? Will that work?'

'I don't know, but it might. It's worth trying.'

Dubiously, Jake put the pellet in a little plastic bag and tucked it into the freezer in the kitchen. Then they waited a nervous half-hour. By then, the bug detector was no longer picking up a signal from it. Jake blew out his cheeks with relief. Magda nodded agreement. They could begin to relax, it seemed.

CHAPTER TWENTY-SEVEN

Moscow

'We lost him.'

'Again?' Blok gave a weary sigh.

'Unfortunately.' Looking grim-faced, Kozlov shrugged and added, 'He has help, plenty of it.'

'Who from?'

Kozlov shook his head.

'The Americans, presumably?' Blok suggested.

'Probably. But we haven't seen them.'

Blok considered. It wasn't good. Heads would roll over this, amongst them conceivably even his own if he couldn't sort it out. He wouldn't mind too much if he was sent back to pasture, but he would much rather leave with a triumph than a failure left behind him. He would also like to have the reward the president had promised him. The money would be very welcome.

More than that, though, he had come to feel he would like his old job back. Sitting in this chair, doing what he used to do, had brought him back to life. He had never felt better. Older he might be, but far from past it. He was younger than the president anyway, and look how well that man was still doing.

He sighed. Kozlov was a problem, an obstacle to his return. Kozlov was awaiting his second departure with poorly hidden impatience. That was perfectly understandable — he wanted his job back — but that made him a problem for Blok, one that would have to be dealt with if he himself were to return here for good. Meanwhile, of course, there was a task to be completed.

'We have to find him, Boris. Tell me what you have on his latest movements.'

'Well, we tracked him to Portugal.'

'Portugal? That's a long way from Montenegro.'

'Even further from Russia,' Kozlov pointed out. 'If we had been involved earlier, he wouldn't have got out of Moscow.'

Blok waved that away irritably. 'Tut-tut, Boris. Then what happened?'

'Off the southern coast of Portugal, there are islands, apparently, many of them. Small islands. He went to one of them.'

'And?'

'Since then we've heard no more.'

'What do you mean?'

'Transmissions ceased.'

'How could that happen?'

Kozlov shrugged. Blok could tell what he was thinking. It wasn't for him to say, General. Things happened, General. He wasn't going to try to guess why, he would wait until the technicians told him, General.

But Blok wasn't prepared to let him off the hook. 'Your best guess, Boris?'

'Technical failure, perhaps?'

It was possible. Blok knew that. He also knew he had been given the easy answer. In effect, Kozlov was admitting he didn't have a clue. Well, he wouldn't hold that against him, for now, because he didn't have a clue either.

'Is he still there, on this island?'

'Possibly. But we don't know that either.'

Blok spun round in his chair to study the wall map of Western Europe.

Portugal? What on earth was he doing there? Blok had to admit he knew next to nothing about the country, essentially because it had never entered the picture during his time in office. It was a nothing country, like Montenegro. Who could have taken him there? And who could take him out of there?

The Americans were the only ones who came to mind. He could think of no one else. Certainly not the Portuguese. They were not players in this game. The French? Or the Germans? Somehow he didn't think so. They couldn't be bothered these days with anything that didn't affect them directly.

The British? Perhaps. They tried to stay in the game, holding on to what was left of their former power by their fingernails, but it was a struggle for them now. So, probably the Americans. They were the ones with the resources, and Bortsov would be a treasure trove to them. Well worth spending some of their riches.

'Let us assume he is still there, on one of these islands, Boris. Technology doesn't lie. That's where he went. We know that at least. Maybe he's just out of range at present. We must search for him, one island after another, until we find him.'

'How badly do we want him?'

Blok sighed. 'He is important, very important. That is all I can tell you.'

'It may be difficult to remove him from the island. Logistics, politics, local sensitivities . . . We are not strong in Portugal.'

'If all else fails, Boris, we will terminate him — and destroy the body. Is that clear enough?'

Kozlov nodded. It was.

CHAPTER TWENTY-EIGHT

Sitting out on the balcony later that evening, Jake said, 'You know, I don't believe it's over.'

Magda gave him a wry smile. 'No? It is for now, surely?'

'Only until the next ferry comes in.'

'Tomorrow morning, then?'

'Tomorrow morning,' he agreed. 'Seriously, perhaps not even that long.'

'What aren't you telling me, Jake?'

He shook his head and sipped his coffee. 'Nothing, I'm not holding anything back. I'm just thinking the ferry won't be the only way to reach the island.'

'That's true.' She thought for a moment. 'Lots of boats in Olhão could bring people across to the island.'

'Exactly. The big question is whether the Russians know where we are.'

'How likely is it, do you think?'

'No idea. I suppose it depends on whether we were in range when the chip stopped sending its message.'

But Jake did have an idea. Now they were here, the island just didn't feel quite as safe as he had hoped it would. After all, they had been tracked all the way across the continent and it was only now that they had discovered and neutralised that damned pellet. Their best hope was that the Russians had fallen so far behind that they had lost the trail before they reached the island.

Then something else occurred to him.

He had been balancing his chair on its two back legs, his feet against the railing of the balcony. Now he lifted his feet and brought the chair down on to the timber deck with a crash.

'Jake!' Magda complained.

'Sorry.'

'What?' she demanded, seeing the look on his face.

'We should have another look at Yuri.'

'To make sure he's sleeping soundly?'

He shook his head. 'It's something Henderson said.'

Magda stared at him, waiting.

'Oh, I don't know!' Jake said with a sigh. 'I was just thinking . . . What if the tracker pellet isn't the only insert Yuri is carrying?'

'Go on,' she urged.

'Henderson said another thing they used to do, back in the good old USSR, was insert a microdot containing information they wanted a courier to carry. It meant the agent could transport the info safely without risk of losing it or having it stolen — and without knowing what it was.'

Magda frowned. 'So what are you thinking?'

Jake shook his head uncertainly. 'Well, a tracker beacon is one thing. A microdot carrying top-secret information is another. Could one pellet do both jobs?'

'I don't know. Perhaps not. But Yuri might disagree, which could be why he didn't want you to destroy the pellet we took out of him.'

'How much does he really know, though?'

Magda slowly shook her head. 'Hard to tell, isn't it? Possibly, the pellet could do two jobs. Then again, Yuri could be carrying a second insert. We'd better check.'

'It's a pity we've knocked him out.'

'That doesn't matter,' Magda said dismissively. 'We don't need him to be conscious. It's probably better if he isn't. He might argue and be un-cooperative.'

Jake thought that was about right. 'Let's do it,' he said.

* * *

They stripped back the quilt and ran the gizmo over the sleeping Bortsov, who was lying on his front, snoring into the pillow.

'Nothing,' Magda said with a disappointed sigh.

'Not necessarily,' Jake said. 'The tracker beacon gives off a signal that this thing picks up. Maybe a microdot doesn't do that. It could just be dormant, doing nothing at all until it's activated. We need to look for signs of another recent wound. Let's turn him over.'

Easier said than done. It helped that Bortsov was still naked. Undressing him would have been a formidable challenge. But, naked or not, he was still a dead weight that took some shifting. Between them, they managed to turn him over and resume their scrutiny.

'Nothing that I can see,' Jake said eventually with a grimace, stepping back. 'Can you see anything?'

Magda shook her head. 'Plenty of scars and bruises, but nothing obvious or recent, apart from where the tracker pellet was located.'

Jake grimaced and started pacing around the room, feeling very frustrated. 'I still could be right,' he insisted stubbornly. 'There could be a microdot somewhere on him.'

Magda shrugged and said, 'Perhaps we need to find out more about microdots.'

'What do you want to know?'

'You know about them?'

'A bit,' he said, nodding. 'I used to be a spy, remember?'

'So tell me about them.'

'Well, they're a way of getting lots of information into or onto a very small space — a pellet, say. You can get the whole of the Bible on to one no more than a millimetre in diameter, for example. Great for people carrying secrets.'

'How can you do that?'

'Special camera, or reduction equipment. Then it can be read under a microscope or else re-enlarged to normal size. I'm not saying we could do it here, but spies have known about microdots, and used them, for more than a century. Other people, too.'

'It's not new technology, then?'

Jake shook his head. 'Old as the hills. No doubt there are modern, hi-tech versions, as well now.'

'If Yuri has one on him, how can we hope to find it if it might only be a millimetre big?' she asked despairingly. 'Or even smaller?'

Jake had no answer for that. 'I don't know. But if he is carrying one, with or without knowing it, that could explain why they want to abduct him rather than kill him.'

'What could the information be, I wonder?'

'Pass. No idea.'

'They'll have thought it was safe,' Magda mused. 'That it couldn't be lost or stolen. Then someone came along and stole the courier.'

'Exactly.'

'So how do we find it?' she asked again.

'I'm not really sure we need to do that. So long as it doesn't emit a signal that allows him to be tracked, we don't need to know anything more about it — it might even be better that way. All we have to do is look after him for another couple of weeks. Then he, and it, becomes Henderson's problem.'

'Still, it would be nice to know what it's all been about,' Magda said wistfully.

Jake wasn't so sure. Knowledge like that could be a dangerous thing to have.

CHAPTER TWENTY-NINE

'What about the pellet in the freezer?' Jake asked. 'Maybe we could find a use for that?'

'Hmm,' Magda said, getting to her feet. 'Coffee?'

'Please.'

She left him to it and retreated to the kitchen. He returned to the vista over the balcony and stared out at what he had thought of as a lake. Only it wasn't one now. It was a glistening expanse of wet sand, with the water still draining fast from it.

That seemed odd. The Mediterranean wasn't supposed to have tides. Then he remembered that this was actually the Atlantic, not the Med, and the Atlantic did have tides. Very big ones. So what he had thought a lagoon was actually a tidal creek. He'd got it wrong. He grimaced. What else might he have got wrong, he wondered? There was bound to be something.

Suddenly, he had it. It was simple, really, once it had occurred to him. It was like magnetism, like north and south poles. That damned pellet that they had dug out of Bortsov was just as capable of leading people away as it was of attracting them. Why hadn't he thought of that before?

* * *

'But I can't just leave him,' Jake said when Magda returned, and he told her what he was thinking.

She put down the two mugs of coffee and stared at him, puzzled. 'Who? Yuri?'

He nodded.

'Of course you can't! Why would you . . . ? Oh, I see what you mean.'

She sat down heavily and stirred her coffee for a few long moments. 'But I could,' she said thoughtfully.

Reaching for his coffee mug, Jake said, 'Yes, you could.'

He hated to put her in this position, but right now there was nothing else for it.

Magda sat there for a few moments more. Then she said briskly, 'I'd better get myself ready. The sooner I go, the better.'

'Are you up for it?'

She nodded. 'Where exactly is the hire car parked? I don't want to take the truck. That's ours. I don't want to risk compromising it — or having anything happen to it.'

He told her where he had left the car. Then he got up and went to fetch the pellet from the freezer.

* * *

She caught the last returning ferry for the day and arrived in Olhão by eight that evening. It felt like the pellet had already defrosted.

Without any problems, she disembarked and located Jake's rental car. Then she set off for Faro. There, she left the car in a long-stay car park and made her way to the railway station, where she bought a ticket to Lisbon on the next train, which was to leave at 22.17. All she had to do after that was wait patiently in a nearby café for an hour.

Given what Jake had told her about the relentless pursuit all the way from Montenegro, it was a bit of an anxious wait. Her nerves as well as her patience were stretched. It was a time to exercise maximum vigilance, yet without

99

appearing to do so. Every new customer entering the café was a potential threat, every male in the vicinity a possible hitman answering the siren call of the pellet.

No! she told herself sharply. That was wrong. Lone men were probably not a threat. From what Jake had said, it was a team, not an individual, pursuing Bortsov. She needed to watch out for males coordinating their movements. But that was wrong, too. If they were any good, they wouldn't look like a team at all.

Her mind turned to something even more basic — what did the Russians really want with Yuri? Was Jake right in believing abduction rather than assassination was their aim? If so, vengeance was not their sole motive, although in the end it seemed unlikely that Yuri would survive. Once they had what they wanted from, or out of, him, they wouldn't just pat him on the back and wish him Godspeed. It would be a bullet in the back of the head — if he was lucky. She knew how they worked and thought.

And what was it that they did want? If it really was a microdot, what could be on it? That was where both reason and guesswork failed her. She knew next to nothing about Yuri, or where he had come from, or what he used to do, so it was impossible to work it out. Something secret and sensitive, presumably, but that covered an infinity of possibilities. All she really knew was that he was special, one of those gifted individuals she had encountered in her life once or twice before. She had realised that soon after first meeting him.

* * *

With a start, she realised she was nearly out of time. Only ten minutes to go. She jumped up and made her way out of the café and along to the platform serving the Lisbon-bound train. Surprisingly, quite a crowd was already gathered there. She stood for a few moments, running her eyes over the faces without seeing anyone or anything suspicious. It could be any of them or none, she decided. Best just to concentrate on surviving the next few minutes. Then her job would be done.

The train arrived, and she climbed aboard, making her way to her designated seat. Sitting down before any other passengers arrived nearby, she slipped the pellet down the back of the seat.

Almost immediately she changed her mind, took it back and planted it somewhere even better.

Then she suddenly clasped her hands to her face, as if in agony or consternation at forgetting something important. She jumped up and made her way to the nearest exit and left the train. Soon afterwards, she left the station.

Taking care to make sure she wasn't followed, she made her way to the main bus station and bought a ticket she wasn't going to use for a late-night bus to a distant town she didn't know and had never even heard of. Then she returned to the hire car and set off in it back the way she had come. Job done.

CHAPTER THIRTY

Blok felt they were entering the end game now. Bortsov was at the far edge of the European continent, with nowhere left to run. He could still fly away, of course, but for some reason the Americans had not used air transport so far. He didn't understand why. Nor did he expect that to change.

That was how these things worked, in his long experience. Handlers tended to stick to their game plan, not least because they didn't like to be told they should have done something different from the outset. They wanted to prove they had been right all along. Kozlov would be like that, unfortunately, if and when he got this job back. Blok didn't have any doubt about that.

Anyway, because Bortsov and his protectors were adhering to their plan, his men ought to be able to catch up with them. Even though they didn't know it, the Americans were proving to be a big help.

* * *

'General, good news!' Kozlov said, bursting into the room to interrupt him. 'We're back on track.'

Blok spun round. 'He's been found?'

Kozlov grinned and nodded.

'So where is he? On one of the islands still?'

'No. Back on the mainland, near Faro.'

Blok grimaced. 'The airport! He's heading there.'

It was not what he had expected, but it was what he had feared. The Americans were going to airlift him out, after all.

'I don't think so,' Kozlov said, shaking his head. 'He's gone past the airport already, and he's travelling further to the west.'

Blok strode over to the wall map and studied the Iberian Peninsula. Where was Bortsov going now? As far as he knew, all those towns along the coast were just tourist resorts. Nothing there for him, unless he was heading for a small airfield. There would be plenty of them, he was sure, for the film stars and billionaires who liked to make their fleeting visits to the Algarve.

'Perhaps he just wants a holiday by the Portuguese seaside,' he joked over his shoulder, 'given how his stay in Budva was . . . interrupted.'

Kozlov smiled dutifully.

Hilarity aside, it was time for a decision. One that Blok had thought he might have to make for some time. Kozlov wouldn't like it, but it was time he got his hands dirty. He had been sitting in offices for far too long.

'I need you there as soon as possible, Boris, to organise things on the ground. Take more men with you. This business has gone on far too long already. We need to bring it to an end, one way or another. The president expects nothing less.'

CHAPTER THIRTY-ONE

Bortsov was hungry when he woke up the next day. Very hungry.

'I must have food,' he told Jake, who had heard him stirring, and had stuck his head round the door to his room.

'How are you feeling?' Jake said, sidestepping the demand.

'Hungry. I want food.'

Jake nodded. 'I heard you the first time. So you're all right?'

Bortsov just glowered.

'Do you want to get dressed first?'

Bortsov tossed the quilt aside and seemed stunned by what he saw. 'My clothes?' he demanded almost hysterically. 'Where are they?'

'In the wash, old boy. Which is where you need to be.'

Jake directed Bortsov's attention to a pile of the new clothing Magda had provided.

'See if there's anything there to fit you while we wait for your own clothes to dry. I suggest taking a shower first, though, as I have done. We were both stinking a bit after our week on the road.'

Bortsov shifted position and winced. 'My . . . Ah!' he said gingerly. 'Now I remember. You and that woman have done something to me.'

'Took something out of you, actually. A tracker pellet — remember?'

Bortsov nodded. 'Where is it?'

'I believe it's on a train heading for Lisbon. At least, that's where Magda told me she put it when she phoned last night.'

'This is a joke?'

Jake shook his head.

'On a railway train?'

'That's right. Like I said, going to Lisbon.'

Bortsov stared at him with incredulity. 'I need it!' he shouted.

'No, you don't. Listen, Yuri. That damned pellet was how they've been tracking us. We talked about it, remember? We had to get rid of it — or we might all have been dead by now!'

Bortsov shook his head. 'You, probably, and the woman. You might both be dead. But not me. I am too valuable.'

With that, he laid back down again — flinching with the pressure on his raw wound — and pulled the pillow over his head. Jake looked askance at him and sighed, working hard at keeping his patience.

'You still think there was valuable information on that pellet?'

'Go away. Go to hell!'

'I'm trying to be kind here, Yuri. Listen to me. We accept that you have valuable information. But we don't believe it is on that pellet.'

'It is. It has to be.'

'No, it doesn't. That pellet is just a tracking beacon.'

'I have nothing else! I never have had. Go here, go there, they say. But they give me nothing to carry. Never!'

'Maybe on a microdot, somewhere else on your body? Have you considered that possibility?'

Bortsov removed the pillow and stared at him for a moment. Seemingly placated, he repeated his demand for food, insisting that he was hungry.

105

'We'll eat when Magda gets back, which won't be long now,' Jake told him. 'She'll be on the first ferry. We'll all eat together.'

'I need food now,' Bortsov said stubbornly.

It was Jake's turn to stare with incredulity. It was like looking after an unreasonable child. Then again, he supposed it had been like that since the very beginning.

'I have diabetes,' Bortsov said. 'I must eat now.'

'No, you don't. There have been no signs of it, and I would have been told if you had. Besides, you have no medication with you, and no signs of injections either. We'll just wait for Magda,' he concluded.

'What time is it?'

'Eight thirty.'

Bortsov groaned and stuck his head under the pillow again.

'While we wait,' Jake suggested again, 'why not have a shower, and then get dressed in clean clothes?'

No response.

Jake turned away in disgust and left him to it. The hell with him!

CHAPTER THIRTY-TWO

The ferry would be in any minute now, Jake mused. Then she would have a ten-minute walk to get here. After that, they could give His Lordship some breakfast and talk about what to do next. Whatever they decided, it was going to be a long two-and-something weeks remaining ahead of them. Bortsov certainly wasn't the easiest person to deal with. A pain in the neck, most of the time. Had been since the start. An arrogant bastard, as well!

Jake gave a rueful smile as he heard the shower start. At least he'd got out of bed. That was a good start. Hopefully, he would be able to dry himself and get dressed as well. He'd seen more than enough of that naked body.

Out on the balcony, he stood and watched as gulls circled endlessly and a welcome breeze ruffled the marram grass across the dunes. A couple of hundred yards away, the rising sun gleamed on the still waters of the lagoon, or tidal creek — or whatever the hell it was!

He was actually happy to be here, he realised, whatever the circumstances. It just felt good. And so peaceful. He dared to hope it would stay that way now that damned pellet was somewhere in Lisbon.

Then he found himself wondering once again what it was that made Bortsov so important — and that, in his own opinion, at least, made him assassination proof. If it was his knowledge of the GRU — or whoever it was that employed him — or if it was to make an example of him, then surely the Russians would just want him dead? They wouldn't bother trying to abduct him. There would be no point. And abduction did seem to be their aim.

The only way it made sense was if Bortsov was carrying something important to both sides. It certainly wasn't papers, plans, files or computer memory sticks in a physical sense. It had to be something like info on a microdot.

So, whatever Yuri thought, however important he believed himself to be, he actually wasn't very important at all. He was a courier, plain and simple. He took stuff across borders and oceans without seeing it, and probably without even knowing anything about it. The lowest of the low in the intelligence world. He was no more than a living envelope.

Jake smiled with delight at the thought. A living envelope! He rather liked that notion. It put his at times insufferable charge in proper perspective.

He might be wrong, of course. The only thing he really knew for sure was that Bortsov had had nothing to do with any failed coup in Montenegro. That suggestion had just been Henderson being fanciful, and typically devious.

* * *

'Anybody home?' a voice cried from the front doorway.

'Only us!' Jake called back, spinning round, a big smile of relief on his face. Magda!

'Any problems?' he asked anxiously.

She shook her head. 'None at all.'

'Thank God for that,' he said, taking her in his arms.

* * *

Over breakfast, Magda confirmed that the pellet abstracted from Bortsov would be in Lisbon by now, and almost certainly there to stay.

'At first, I tucked it behind the seat. Then I realised that meant it would just come back to Faro when the train returned. So I put it in a rubbish container instead.'

'Good thinking,' Jake said with an appreciative grin.

'So it should be gone for ever,' Magda concluded, 'unless the Russians manage to recover it from a landfill site or an incinerator.'

Jake chuckled.

Bortsov didn't. He looked annoyed.

'Cheer up!' Jake told him. 'All that thing did was tell them where you were.'

'Perhaps.'

'For sure. There's no way it could have contained information. It was just a tracking device.'

Bortsov shrugged and helped himself to more sliced ham and cheese.

'Yuri, I'm not saying you have one, but do you have any idea where such a thing as a microdot could have been implanted on you?' Magda asked.

'No.'

'None at all?'

He shook his head.

'Of course, it wouldn't have to be on him personally, would it?' Jake said thoughtfully. 'It could be on something he brought with him.'

'That would be a bit risky, wouldn't it?' Magda pointed out.

'I suppose it would. There would be no guarantee that something he was carrying would make it. He could lose it. Somebody could steal it. Anything!' he added with a shrug.

'But not if it's actually on him,' Magda said, gazing at Yuri speculatively.

Bortsov said nothing. He just continued chewing his way through the pile of food he had assembled on his plate.

That was his focus now. He was oblivious to people talking about him — and deciding things about him. He was used to that.

'It might help,' Jake said, trying to be conciliatory, 'if we knew what the information was about. Then we would know if the Russians need to get it back or if they just want to stop our side, the Americans basically, getting it. Can you help us there, Yuri?'

'No.'

'Can't? Or won't?'

'No.'

'That's helpful,' Jake murmured, smiling to hide his exasperation. 'What about where a microdot might be located? Are you sure you can't help us there either, Yuri?'

'I want some more coffee,' Bortsov said, fixing his eyes on Magda.

'It's over there.' She nodded towards the kitchen counter. 'Go and get it.'

Bortsov narrowed his eyes, as if about to make his request an order. Then he thought better of it, nodded and got up to pour himself more coffee from the flask.

'I can tell you this much,' he said conversationally as he sat back down. 'This thing you talk about, this microdot, if it exists, it is not on anything I carry or have brought with me. I know that because now I have nothing I started out with. Everything I had is gone — clothes, suitcase, wallet, everything! Now I am homeless, and a vagabond only.'

'That was quite a speech. But you're not only a vagabond,' Jake told him tartly. 'You're also a first-class—'

'Everything, Yuri?' Magda leaned forward urgently to interrupt. 'Are you sure? Everything is really gone?'

'Everything.'

She thought for a moment and then said, 'In that case, how did you cross the borders when you came through Montenegro, Bosnia and Herzegovina, Croatia and into Italy?'

'By car,' Bortsov said dismissively.

'Those countries are not in the EU. How did you get past the border guards? What did you show them?'

'What do you think?' he responded with contempt. 'My passport!'

'Your passport?'

'Of course. Like everybody else.'

'The passport given to you in Russia?'

Bortsov didn't bother with what he clearly thought was a stupid question.

Magda turned to look at Jake, who said quietly, 'That's it, then, isn't it? It's on his passport.'

CHAPTER THIRTY-THREE

Bortsov, behaving helpfully for once, produced his passport and handed it over for inspection. Jake glanced at it and immediately realised the enormity, impossibility even, of the task he had set himself.

'It can't be done without an extremely powerful microscope,' he soon announced with a sigh. 'There must be millions of dots on this thing.'

Bortsov shrugged as if he had expected no other conclusion.

Jake looked at Magda, who said, 'I have nothing to say. Such matters are beyond my understanding.'

'And mine, too,' Jake said, with a rueful grin.

'Does it matter?' Magda added. 'Would it make any difference if we could find a microdot — if there is one?'

'No, not really,' Jake admitted with a sigh. 'We couldn't read it, anyway. Our job is to look after Yuri. Let's just concentrate on that.'

Bortsov moved his head up and down in agreement. 'That is true,' he said. 'But at least now I know something I didn't know before. You have told me about these things called microdots.'

'Is that it, though?' Jake frowned. 'Is there really a microdot on your passport?'

'I believe there could be. It was impressed on me that I must not lose the passport or allow anyone else to have it. I was surprised at the time that such things were said. Now I can understand why.'

'Any chance of you letting us know what information there might be?'

'None.' Bortsov sat up straight and looked even more serious. 'There would be no point, anyway. I think you and Magda are not military engineers.'

'Is that what you are — an engineer?'

'No comment,' Bortsov said infuriatingly. 'I will tell you nothing more. It is not necessary, and it will be of no use.'

CHAPTER THIRTY-FOUR

Being rid of Kozlov left Blok free to concentrate and think without frequent interruptions from a man who was resentful, understandably so, of his predecessor's return to office and command of the department. Being sent to Portugal would also be good for Kozlov, Blok decided. It would give him something purposeful to do, and the opportunity to re-establish himself as a power in the department. So, good all round, Blok thought with satisfaction.

He returned to the matter at hand. What was Bortsov up to? Where were his helpers taking him?

One of the technicians came with up an answer. 'It looks like he's heading for Lisbon, General.'

'Ah! That makes more sense. So, he isn't looking for a trip to the seaside?'

'No, sir.' Emboldened by the General's evident good humour, the technician added, 'One thing that's a surprise is that he's not travelling on the main highway, the A22, or E01 as it's also called. He's not far from it, but perhaps he's on minor roads to avoid detection. The main roads have technology — cameras and computers — to identify and record cars and their drivers, I believe.'

Blok glanced at the plot the technician had brought with him, showing the pattern of beacon signals, and then looked again at the wall map.

'No. He's not in a car,' he concluded.

He traced a line on the map with his index finger. 'This is a railway. He's travelling by train now.'

CHAPTER THIRTY-FIVE

Over the next few days, life settled into a gentle rhythm.
Like Bortsov, Jake caught up on some sleep. His bruises and
memories from what had been an exhausting and harrowing
journey began to fade, and some of the tension left him too.
Bortsov seemed happy to stay indoors, while Jake and Magda
alternated in venturing outside to feel the sun on their backs.
But always, one of them would be in the house with him,
day or night.

They established a little routine. Either Jake or Magda
would visit the island's little convenience store each morning to pick up food and other items they needed. Then they
would take turns monitoring the incoming ferries, keeping
an eye out for visitors who didn't seem to belong and might
possibly be a threat. It wasn't a foolproof approach, but it
was something to occupy them and keep them on their toes.

Jake was well aware of the need for vigilance. Although
sending the tracker on a magical mystery tour would have
bought them some time, it was still a dangerous game they
were playing, and they were up against some of the world's
best. Sooner or later, the people hunting Bortsov were going
to realise or guess that the beacon they were tracking was
no longer on his person. When that happened, they would

reverse their route until they reached the point at which something out of the ordinary had happened, after which the contact had no longer been firm. Then the hunt would resume.

He had little doubt that they would identify Olhão as the turning point, or that once they did, their eyes would turn to the offshore islands. They would still have plenty to do, but Armona, as the biggest of the islands, would soon receive their attention. After that, it would just be a matter of time, and what resources they were able to deploy.

Put like that, Jake thought with a grimace, surviving for another ten or twelve days on Armona didn't seem such a safe bet after all. The hunters would be back in the chase with a chance, a very good chance, of bringing it to a successful conclusion.

* * *

Magda shook her head as she joined him on the balcony after her morning excursion. 'Nothing,' she said.

Jake nodded. 'Good.'

'Where's Yuri? I've bought him some of that rye bread he likes so much.'

'In his room, I think.'

'You *think*, Jake?' Magda glared.

He held up his hand apologetically. 'Sorry! You're right. I should know.'

He got up out of the basket chair, suddenly aware how easily complacency could overtake them, bearing in mind he'd just been thinking about how easily the Russians could catch up.

So, of course, when Jake went to investigate, Bortsov wasn't in his room. He wasn't anywhere in the house. Jake grew annoyed. With himself and with Bortsov. Not good enough. They had impressed on him that he couldn't go wandering out alone — if that was what he had done. And Jake had let him.

He went outside to look around the little garden surrounding the house. No Bortsov. Magda came out to join him.

'Any luck?'

'I don't know where he is,' Jake admitted. 'I'm going to look for him.'

'I'll stay here,' Magda said. 'One of us should. He might be worried if he comes back and finds no one in the house.'

'Not as worried as he'll be when I find him!' Jake snapped. 'I told him . . .'

'Leave it, Jake! No threats. Just find him.'

CHAPTER THIRTY-SIX

It was so out of character for Yuri to go missing that Jake had to fight hard against the gnawing anxiety in the pit of his stomach. It was out of character for him to go anywhere! Jake had given up trying to cajole or order him outside for some exercise. The man just hadn't been interested. Until now.

So, where the hell was he?

Thinking he might have gone shopping, Jake walked the length of the main pathway in both directions without seeing Bortsov in any of the handful of shops and cafes. Nor was he hanging around the ferry terminal.

Next, boiling with frustration, Jake looked around a tidal pool where a handful of boats were kept, again without success. The beach, then, at the end of the boardwalk? That was no good either. Nor did he find his man sheltering beneath the parasols of either of the beach bars, out across the burning white sand.

The possibilities were not exhausted, but the ones that were left would require a lot more effort to search. Jake didn't feel much like tackling them, and he doubted Bortsov would have done either. He wasn't an athletic, outdoorsy sort of person, and a mile or two over soft sand in the heat wouldn't be an attractive option even for sun worshippers.

What about the old military base? Jake wondered speculatively. It was well kept and secure, even if it wasn't in use now. Could he have gone there for whatever reason? Unlikely. There was no outstanding reason for him to have done so, unless it was for the sheer nostalgia of seeing security fencing, barbed wire and warning notices. If anyone would miss those, it might be Bortsov.

The base was only a couple of hundred yards beyond the end of the pathway. Jake decided it was worth a short excursion to check. He was running out of ideas, anyway.

From a distance, the base looked to be totally abandoned, a relic perhaps of the Cold War all those years ago. Close up, Jake could see that it wasn't quite like that. A radar tower was still operating, and the buildings and security fence were all in good repair. Mothballed, rather than abandoned, he decided. A communications base that had been de-manned and perhaps left on automatic control, but that could soon be manned up again if the need ever arose.

He walked around the perimeter fence anyway, hearing a faint electrical hum from somewhere inside the compound but without seeing any signs of human presence. Unless Bortsov had developed an urgent need to contact someone in the outside world using sophisticated military equipment, he wasn't going to be here.

Back where he'd started, Jake stood for a moment and looked around. What to do? Where to go next?

He was really worried now. Not panicking — yet — but the heat wasn't the only reason he was sweating heavily. He was beginning to think the unthinkable. Had Bortsov been snatched? Were the Russians here already?

No, he didn't believe that. Not really. Not yet.

Damn you, Yuri! I don't need this. Where the hell are you, man?

He was knackered. He stood still on the spot and turned round, gazing in all directions. Surprisingly, just a short distance away, there was a small patch of woodland, a pinewood, that he hadn't really noticed before. Curious, wondering how that could have developed, he made his way across the sand towards it.

* * *

That was where he found Bortsov. All he could tell at first was that it was a body. He grimaced and swore aloud, and started jogging towards where the body lay under the trees. Already, he was almost resigned to what he expected to find. It seemed to fit.

Yet, when he was a few yards away, the body moved and sat up. Jake stopped and stared with mixed relief and shock.

'Yuri! What the hell?' he gasped, his heart pounding now as if he had been sprinting.

'Hello, Jake. So you found me?'

The shock gave way to pure relief. Jake scarcely knew what to say.

'Are you all right, Yuri?' he managed. 'What on earth are you doing here? We were worried about you.'

'I wanted to see the trees.'

'The trees?' Jake looked around as Bortsov raised his arms to encompass all the pinewood.

'You'd noticed them?'

'Of course.' Yuri nodded and smiled. 'Pine trees, like at home. I could see them from the window of my room.'

So that was what it was about, Jake thought grimly. A touch of homesickness. He'd never thought of that. He'd never believed the man was even capable of such a feeling.

'You should have said, Yuri. I've been all over the bloody island, looking for you. I'm damn near worn out!'

'Sorry, Jake.' He even sounded as if he meant it.

Jake gave a weary smile and flopped down beside him. 'It doesn't matter now. You're all right. That's the main thing.'

They were quiet for a while. Then Jake asked, 'How are you doing, Yuri? Really?'

'Good.' Bortsov laid back down and stared up into the branches gently swaying and rustling overhead. 'I like it here.'

'Yes. It's nice,' Jake admitted, even though the wood wasn't really what he'd been thinking about.

But it was very pleasant. The trees gave shade as well as their aromatic scent and gentle whispering sound.

'I know you're wondering why I'm here, Jake, like this?'

'No, Yuri. You've already told me. It's nice here, a nice place.'

Yuri shook his head. 'I mean with you and Magda . . . Why I am running away from my homeland.'

'It had crossed my mind,' Jake admitted.

'It is to save lives, Jake. My life, yes, of course. Also, the lives of many other people. I had to leave Russia. I could do nothing there to help people, but here, in the West, perhaps I can.'

Jake doubted that. He didn't wish to disturb the mood but, having spent a very long couple of weeks in Yuri's company, he doubted that very much indeed. Still, Giles Henderson was no fool, and he seemed very sure of Yuri's value. Who was he to doubt the judgement of a man like Henderson?

'Not long to go now, Yuri,' he said gently. 'Stay calm. The people to help you will be here soon.'

God willing! he thought a little despairingly. The pressure was getting to him a bit, and at that moment it felt more likely that they had been forgotten about, abandoned even. Yuri Bortsov, far from helping to save the world, would have become yet another lost soul on a fool's errand. And where would that leave him? he wondered. And his darling Magda?

CHAPTER THIRTY-SEVEN

Left alone, Blok returned to study the wall map once more. What was Bortsov doing now? he wondered. Was he really going, or being taken, to Lisbon? Why? And what then?

All he had, really had, were questions. It was so frustrating. He hadn't been brought back to think up more questions. His reputation was as a problem solver, and a creative thinker, not a dull plodder like Kozlov.

At least, it always had been, he thought ruefully. Perhaps he was over the hill now, too old, and the president had overestimated his remaining abilities? Maybe all his old skills, talents were gone now, leaving him as yet another person who could see only questions and problems, without seeing answers.

The question continued to nag at him. Then he frowned as yet another issue arose in his mind. How likely was this journey of Bortsov's? Lisbon? What was the point of that?

The Americans could have airlifted him out long before now, long before he even reached Portugal. So, what was going on? What were they thinking?

He returned to his desk, sat down and twiddled the pen he found there, turning it over and over between his fingers as he continued to stare at the wall map, but not really seeing it now. Other images were in his head, some of them associated with long train journeys, others with travelling through hot, dry countries.

'Damn!' he said, suddenly sitting up straight. 'Damn, damn, damn!'

Why hadn't he seen it before now? Whatever made him think Bortsov would have abandoned car travel in favour of a railway train? The one gives unlimited flexibility; the other is akin to a mobile trap. Why would Bortsov give up the freedom of movement that has served him so well?

He reached for the phone and called Kozlov, who was in transit.

'Boris, the tracking system tells us that the target is heading for Lisbon by railway train.'

'That makes sense, General. Rail travel is fast and uncomplicated, and it will be easier to move him out of the country from Lisbon.'

'All that is true, Boris, but I'm not sure it's the right conclusion to reach. Going to Lisbon doesn't make much sense to me. Nor does travelling by train. It may be what is happening, of course, but it is also possible that it's not. All we really know is that the tracker beacon is heading towards Lisbon by train. That doesn't mean Bortsov is going with it.'

'General, how could that be . . . ?'

'I don't know. But the thought opens up other possibilities. I want us to hedge our bets. Let's split the team. One half can go to Lisbon. The other half should stay with you for the time being.'

'In Faro?'

'No, no! I don't believe there will be anything there for us. Go to . . . Olhão, is it?'

'Olhão, yes.'

'My hunch — and that's all it is — is that we should spend more time looking for him on those islands. I believe he may still be there.'

CHAPTER THIRTY-EIGHT

'You were right, General,' Kozlov said. 'The Lisbon team found the train. The beacon was still transmitting, even though the train was empty and in darkness. They watched as cleaners arrived and began doing their work. Then the beacon started transmitting from a van that was leaving the station. They followed the van.'

'And?' Blok demanded impatiently.

'It went directly to a big municipal refuse-sorting plant. General, the beacon has somehow become detached from our target.'

It was more or less what he had come to expect, and not worth considering further.

'Well, Boris, the technicians here have been studying the record of transmissions from the beacon in great detail. When the beacon left the island, it was taken to the railway station at Faro, where it boarded a train. From what you say, though, it looks as if Bortsov did not go with it. We believe he is still on one of the islands off Olhão. And that's where you should go immediately, Colonel. Recall the team from Lisbon and have them join you in Olhão.'

At last, Blok thought with satisfaction after switching off the phone, we are getting somewhere. Bortsov is pinned down.

CHAPTER THIRTY-NINE

It wasn't much. The signs were few and subtle. But they were enough. It was time to go.

'We need to move,' Jake said to Magda when he returned from the convenience shop.

'Move?'

'We can't stay here.'

Magda put down the tea towel and the dish she was drying. She turned to stare at him. Jake was gazing back over his shoulder, through the half-open door.

'What did you see?' she demanded.

He turned back to her. 'I think they've probably found us. At least, they're on the island.'

'What did you see?' she repeated.

Jake looked down at the loaf of bread he was carrying and stepped forward to place it on the kitchen table.

'Not much,' he admitted. 'Just a few little things. I watched a couple of men going up and down paths, obviously searching for something — or someone. They were being very systematic, going cottage by cottage.'

'From the local council, perhaps?'

'Maybe, but I think not. They looked like strangers. I watched them talking to the gardeners, ask them questions.'

The island had its own parish council, or the equivalent. Men and women dressed in brown uniforms with yellow markings swept the paths and tended to planted areas that were not private gardens.

'Anything else?' Magda asked.

Jake closed the door and turned to face her again, more focused now. 'I saw three pairs of men doing that. They didn't look like single men on holiday. They didn't look Portuguese either. They looked like Northern Europeans, Russians even.'

Magda shrugged. 'Tourists, visitors, perhaps? Looking for accommodation.'

'They would go through the tourist information office, surely?'

'Probably,' she admitted. 'Anything else?'

'The first morning ferry hasn't arrived yet. So how have they got here?'

Magda didn't bother replying. The answer was obvious. If they hadn't come by ferry, either they had their own boat or they had paid a private boat owner to bring them. There were plenty of boat owners on the quayside in Olhão offering that service, but you would need to be in a hurry or have plenty of money to be prepared to pay what they would charge. It was unlikely that you would be a holidaymaker with all the time in the world.

Jake hadn't finished yet. He stood by the big window, gazing out towards the main path.

'Two of the men passed close by me,' he said. 'I'm pretty sure they were talking in Russian. I don't know the language, but it was certainly Eastern European, and I heard one or two words I know. Most of all, I recognised their delivery, their intonation — that low, rumbling sound without inflection that to me is Russian.'

Magda sat down heavily on a chair. 'If you're right,' she said, looking deeply concerned, 'it is very worrying. We need to prepare.'

CHAPTER FORTY

A lingering concern of Blok's was the realisation that he might just be wrong about the help Bortsov was being given, and hence, his ultimate destination. Perhaps it had nothing to do with the Americans? It could be that the reason he was in Portugal, and possibly heading for Lisbon, was that Brazil was where he was going. After all, Brazil was a very big country, and the main Portuguese-speaking country in the world. Easy to get lost there.

But surely it couldn't be the Portuguese who were helping him? What would be in it for them?

He shook his head and returned to working his way back through the records of Bortsov's flight, looking to see if he had missed anything. It didn't look like it. Everything was plain and uncomplicated until Bortsov, and whoever it was that was helping him, reached Olhão and set off for the off-shore islands. Soon after that, the transmissions stopped for a while. It must have been then that the beacon was discovered and perhaps removed.

When transmissions began again, there was a different pattern. That was obvious now. It was no longer the chaotic, almost random, pattern exhibited as Bortsov followed country roads and tried to avoid express routes. Instead, the line was straight as a die, heading fast and direct to Lisbon. There was no doubt about it. Olhão was where things had changed.

Now things were changing for him too, Blok thought with a grimace. There was pressure from the president's office, gentle so far, but insidious and building. The president wanted this matter resolved — and soon. He wasn't impressed with progress so far.

The focus had shifted too. Presidential interest had faded in playing the long game and wringing out everything they could about this defection. Now, it was all about preventing the information Bortsov carried reaching the Americans, or anyone else for that matter. The new focus was on stopping him from going any further. Whatever it took.

Realpolitik, Blok thought with a philosophical shrug. Well, he could change focus, too. He could accept that all that really mattered now was preventing an information avalanche in the wrong direction. The rest of it didn't really matter very much, after all.

He reached for the phone and called Kozlov yet again with revised orders, this time the ones that Kozlov had wanted all along. Bortsov was to be eliminated by any means possible. Then the team should be split up, and its members make their separate and unobtrusive ways back home.

CHAPTER FORTY-ONE

After Kozlov's team had spent several fruitless days searching the islands of the Ria Formosa Park, Blok became worried. Was he wrong? Had Bortsov given them the slip yet again?

The trouble was that Kozlov was the wrong man to be in charge of ground operations in Portugal, or anywhere else, for that matter. Blok simply didn't rate him. He had wanted Kozlov as far away from himself as possible, but now Kozlov was proving a handicap out in the field too. He would probably continue to be that wherever he was, now and in the future. It was time to do something about it.

Blok contacted Sergeant Igor Radowski, a long-term and ultra-loyal associate, and met him in a small park a little distance from the Kremlin. There were few formalities governing their meeting. Theirs was a working relationship that had served them both well in the North Caucasus and sundry other places.

'Good to see you again, General!' Radowski said with a smile, getting up from the park bench as Blok approached.

'And you, Igor. Come, walk with me. How goes it?'

'Well, I suppose. Not like it was when you were in charge, though, General, but I can't complain too much.'

'Good man! Igor, you know about this operation ongoing in Portugal?'

'Yes, General.'

'I want you to join it. Get out there as soon as you can. I'll tell Colonel Kozlov to expect you.'

'Colonel Kozlov?' Radowski said, sounding and looking a little puzzled. 'He is there now? In charge, presumably? That seems a little unusual.'

'I know, I know! He's too old and without significant experience in the field. He's a desk man, right?'

Radowski shrugged but declined to comment further.

'I want you to know that Kozlov is not to survive this mission. With him gone, you will be in charge.' Blok waited a heartbeat or two before adding, 'Is that clear?'

Radowski nodded now and smiled. 'It's like that, is it, General?'

'It is. He is not the right man to head the operation, or this department either, for that matter. That has become abundantly clear — both to myself and to others much higher up in the Kremlin. It has been decided. He must go.'

'What will happen then, General, may I ask? After this operation is concluded, I mean?'

'I believe you will see me return to run the department for at least a time, Igor. On a permanent basis, that is. Retirement hasn't really suited me.'

With a broad smile now, Radowski said, 'That will be good, General, very good. I look forward to that happening.'

They shook hands. It was a deal.

Then, before they parted, Blok said, 'I don't care what sort of accident Kozlov has, by the way, but it would be better if it were soon. His presence in Portugal is not helping things there. Nor is it helping me here. Get rid of Kozlov, and then your mission will be to eliminate the traitor Bortsov.'

'Understood, General.'

CHAPTER FORTY-TWO

It was hot that night. And humid. The heat had built up during the day and there had been no breeze to disperse it. Something was coming. Perhaps a storm. Something, anyway. And soon. But not yet, perhaps.

Sleep was difficult and would have been even without the sultry conditions. As it was, Jake had lain awake for several hours before he heard it. Not much. Just furtive sounds that might have been made by four-legged night creatures on the prowl. He swung his legs aside, touched the floor with his toes and got to his feet. Something, or nothing? He had to know.

His careful movement had still woken Magda. 'What is it?' she whispered.

'I don't know. Something.'

Slipping away, he headed quietly out of the room without turning on any lights, making for the kitchen at the back of the house. On the way, he picked up an axe handle. He had found it in the little shed attached to the house and placed it close at hand. It was heavy wood and made a good club.

Pausing for a moment when he reached the door, he stood still, listening intently. Whatever had woken him, he couldn't hear it now. But he trusted his instincts and senses and knew he hadn't imagined the sounds.

He crossed to the window and from the edge of the blind, without moving it, he looked out. Not pitch black out there. More dark, gloomy. Nothing moving. Nothing out of place either, so far as he could see.

Returning to the bedroom, he pulled on a shirt and some trousers. Then he crept into the living room. Nothing there either, and in Yuri's room, only Yuri, sleeping soundly.

Then, looking out from the living-room window, he saw shadowy movement in the near distance. It was enough. He spun round to Magda, who had followed him into the room.

'They're here!' he snapped. 'Get dressed.'

Next, he woke Yuri, who stared blankly up at him.

'Your friends have arrived,' Jake said tersely. 'You need to dress. We have to get out.'

He left Yuri to get ready and returned to the living-room window. From there, he could see now that there was movement around a neighbouring cottage. He saw several figures flitting through the darkness. It looked like they had narrowed their search down to the immediate area but not the actual cottage. They would probably be searching each house in turn.

He moved away from the window and turned to see Magda and Yuri waiting for him in the kitchen doorway. They were holding the emergency backpacks that had been prepared in advance and put ready. He took his from Magda and led the way to the back door. Nothing was said. Nothing needed to be said. The situation they had anticipated had arrived. It was time to go — if they could.

CHAPTER FORTY-THREE

Thankfully, there was nobody waiting for them at the back of the cottage. Jake closed the door quietly and led the way across the small patch of garden and onto the rough, overgrown ground beyond. It was difficult going in the dark, but it had to be done. There was no other way they could have gone.

The plan, such as it was, was to survive until morning — if they possibly could — and then catch the early ferry back to the mainland — if they could! Jake had ruled out the option of stealing a small boat or persuading the owner of one to transport them. It seemed too risky. Anyone left to watch the moored boats at the ferry terminal would know instantly who they were, and that would be that. The ferry itself was a safer option. They could split up to board it and then mingle with the other passengers, instead of operating as a group.

Jake wondered how many men the Russians had. Quite a few, it seemed. There had been several around the neighbouring cottage. Was that all of them? Probably not. Best to assume there were more. He grimaced at the thought. Given how small the island was, it was going to be hard to avoid detection in the hours before the first ferry arrived.

* * *

They took shelter in a ruined cabin not far from the ferry terminal, just before the long-awaited storm arrived. One end of the building still had a roof. They huddled under that and watched and listened as lightning turned night into day, time and time again, and as heavy rain and thunder put a stop to all conversation for minutes on end.

When the heavy bombardment ceased at last and the storm had become no more than a steady rain, Jake urged the others to try and get some sleep while he kept watch. He didn't believe sleep would be possible, but at least they would be resting. That was something. It would also allow him to listen and give him time to think.

'They won't find us now,' he said more confidently than he actually felt — and more for Yuri's sake than Magda's. 'They missed their chance.'

He didn't really believe that. Nor, he was sure, would Magda. As for Yuri, he thought with a wry inner smile, who could tell what Yuri believed?

After just a few minutes, Magda said, 'I know it is still raining, Jake, but it is not good here. We should move, I think.'

Jake had wondered about that himself. A roof overhead was a good thing in a storm, but . . .

'They will look here,' Yuri contributed. 'This place will be very obvious to them, and they will come here.'

'OK. I agree. Let's move.'

So, they left the ruined cabin, heads ducked against the continuing light rain. They headed further along the shore, finding refuge beneath a clump of tamarisk trees on the edge of a lagoon, where resting fishing boats bobbed up and down unperturbed. They settled down there as best they could to wait for dawn and the early ferry for Olhão.

* * *

Remarkably, Bortsov went to sleep. Jake didn't, and he knew even before she spoke that Magda didn't either. The storm had moved on, but they were wet now and feeling the chill in its aftermath. Discomfort was one thing, but tension had got to them, too. Sleep was impossible. Jake knew they had had one lucky escape that night. They couldn't count on another. They needed to stay alert.

He believed now that he had underestimated the Russians in their determined pursuit. All that had been won by coming here to Armona had been a few days' respite. The hunt hadn't stopped. The Russians hadn't given up. They obviously wanted Yuri very badly indeed.

Still, the brief opportunity to rest and recover had done them all some good. Boy, had they needed that! Now, though, they needed to move on. There were still a few days to go before Henderson took charge of Yuri. Days to endure, and hopefully survive. Right now, he hadn't a clue as to how they were going to do that, or if it would even be possible.

For a start, he had serious doubts about whether they could reach the mainland. The Russians seemed to have more people here than they had put in the field so far, and it was a very, very small island. Surviving long enough just to reach the ferry was going to be a stiff challenge and surviving the crossing and whatever awaited on the other side, an even bigger one. He grimaced as he thought about it.

Yet nothing had really changed. Once more, as ever, they were going to be travelling hopefully.

Where to, though? Not a city or big town. It would be too difficult to stay safe in a place flooded with people. Better to be somewhere quiet, where it was possible to see what was coming at you.

Somewhere in the Alentejo, perhaps? The deep interior of Portugal was empty country, with plenty of villages and small towns that time had forgotten. Somewhere there might be good for them. Where, though? Where, exactly? No idea. He didn't know the region well enough.

'Jake,' Magda whispered, as if reading his thoughts. 'Where shall we go?'

He shook his head. 'Just thinking about that. I'm not sure.'

'You don't know?'

He was loath to admit it, but he really didn't know. Anyway, getting off the island was a more immediate problem. If they managed that, then hopefully something would turn up. They would find somewhere to go, somewhere safe. He was an optimist. He could still believe that.

Not their villa on the edge of São Brás, though. That was private, their safe place that no one in England, not even Giles Henderson, knew about. And he wanted to keep it that way.

'What about Pena again?' Magda whispered.

Pena? He hadn't thought of that. But now he did think about it, his interest grew quickly. It was remote enough. Not too far away. Empty country out there. Just a pity that the old cottage had been destroyed, burnt out by the gangsters pursuing himself and Magda the previous year.

'Pena?'

'I know somewhere we could stay.'

'It got burnt down last year, remember?'

'Somewhere else,' she said. 'There is another cottage.'

'Oh? The same sort of place?'

'Yes, just the same.'

He knew what that meant. Simple, long-neglected, if not actually abandoned altogether.

'It's a possibility, then,' he admitted.

Another cottage, eh? Jake smiled to himself, ruefully acknowledging that there was still so much he didn't know about Magda. She continued to surprise him.

* * *

The hours pressed on, and Jake sat and wondered how the Russians had managed to trace them to Armona. It might not have been too difficult, now he thought about it. Magda putting the tracker pellet on the Lisbon train had won them a day or two, but eventually the ruse would have been discovered. Perhaps when the pellet led them to a landfill site, or when it had travelled a long way in a suspiciously straight line — like a railway line.

Then they would have worked backwards through the sighting log, looking for divergence from the previous pattern of behaviour. Sooner or later they would have got back to Olhão. Then they would have seen that the pellet had travelled offshore before stopping transmitting for a few hours. Eureka!

It was a pity he hadn't found the damned thing earlier. They could have got rid of it a lot sooner, and then Armona would have been the perfect refuge he had hoped it would be. Now it was a bloody trap.

No good thinking like that, though. They were where they were — and they were not without hope. Not at all! If they could actually reach the mainland, the Russians would no longer be able to track them. And for the first time since all this had started, they would have a real chance. How wonderful that would be.

First, though, they had to stay alive long enough to escape from Armona.

CHAPTER FORTY-FOUR

Soon after first light, and well before the sun came up, a man boarded a little fishing boat in the lagoon. Watching him sort a few things out as he prepared for his day's work, Jake realised this could be the answer to his prayers. God, I'm so slow! he thought. He got to his feet and dusted sand from the seat of his trousers. Magda looked up at him questioningly.

'I'm going to see if I can get us a ride. The ferry could be difficult.'

She followed his gaze and nodded. 'Take care!' she urged.

The fisherman glanced round at him without much interest as Jake approached. Reluctantly, and with a surly look, he responded to Jake's greeting. He didn't like being interrupted, it seemed. Not this early in the day. He didn't like being accosted and importuned, either. He shook his head and kept saying no to Jake's request to be run shore.

It was the sight of a big bundle of euros that persuaded him to think again. That did it. He stopped what he was doing with the engine, straightened up and visibly began to change his mind. At the firm offer of two hundred euros, without further debate or negotiation, he wiped his hands on an oily rag and nodded agreement. Jake handed over the money and turned to beckon the others.

The fisherman had very little English and was by nature taciturn — he and Bortsov might have been best mates in another life. Jake knew some Portuguese, but he had no wish to engage beyond the necessary. So conversation was minimal, which suited both parties perfectly.

Magda, who had a lot more Portuguese, kept a pragmatic silence, seeing how things were and having no wish to risk disturbing the business agreement.

'Olhão?' the fisherman queried, looking at Jake for confirmation.

'Olhão. The main harbour.'

'Fast?'

Jake nodded. They couldn't leave Armona quick enough, as far as he was concerned. The others, too, he was sure.

* * *

No one appeared to watch them leave the island, but Jake took little satisfaction from that. The Russians had shown such tenacity and perseverance that he couldn't allow himself to be overly optimistic about their chances of getting away clean and evading pursuit. Sooner or later, he expected them to work out what had happened, and to respond effectively. He just hoped they could stay ahead of the chasing pack until the cavalry arrived.

There was a chill in the air out over the water, and a thin mist that he welcomed as they slid into it.

'Cold!' Magda whispered, screwing up her face and giving a dramatic little shiver.

'Shh!' Jake responded theatrically. 'Don't let Yuri know.'

'I am cold, too,' Bortsov said flatly. 'But I choose not to admit it.'

Magda grinned and said, 'Because you are—'

Jake pressed her arm hard to stop her saying *Russian*. He shook his head when she glanced at him with a wince. 'Best not to say it,' he told her, nodding towards the fisherman.

'Oh, of course,' she said, grimacing. 'I wasn't thinking.'

The less the fisherman knew about them, the better.

That he'd had three passengers, rather than only two, might be a help when the Russians came calling. It might confuse them and win a little time, but not much if he said that one of the three was Russian.

Jake gave Magda a hug. He did sympathise with her. It was cold. Or, rather, they were cold. Having been wet through for several hours was the reason for it, not the temperature. They needed to get out of the mist and have the sun on their backs.

The fisherman, of course, was impervious to weather. Whatever it was like, he had his job to do, anyway. Today he would be late starting, but otherwise it would be a normal day for him. So he was dressed in the jeans and t-shirt he usually wore.

The crossing took half an hour. At the end of it, Jake made sure they were dropped off in the huge working harbour of the port, rather than the ferry landing outside it. They disembarked amongst the trawlers and small fishing boats, reassuringly close to the jetty for the maritime police and military vessels. It was a busy place, already hard at work, and they were far more inconspicuous here than they would have been at the still-deserted ferry landing.

The hire car was where Magda had left it, in the big car park alongside the harbour. They walked past it without hesitation, and with scarcely a glance, making for Jake's old truck. That was where Magda had parked it, on waste ground off a side street a couple of blocks away.

'The car was the only possible link to Yuri and me,' Jake said to Magda. 'They know nothing about you or the truck.'

She nodded agreement. 'So we have broken the link. Now they will have no trail to follow.'

Acknowledging the truth of that statement gave Jake much satisfaction. At last, they were free — for now, at least.

Bortsov sniffed when he saw the vehicle they were to travel in. Clearly, he had envisaged a bit more luxury than the truck could offer.

'Just get in,' Jake snapped. 'Where we're going, the truck will be a lot better than any car.'

'If you say so,' Bortsov responded.

Jake was about to bite his head off when Magda nudged him. It had been a long night for all of them. No point responding to yet another disagreeable tantrum from their little troublemaker. It was a mystery to him why the Russians wanted Bortsov back — he would have thought they would be partying to celebrate having got rid of him.

It was not yet seven in the morning, but Olhão was busy. The streets around the port were clogged with traffic and the main road to Faro was carrying a dense stream of cars and trucks, wagons and vans. The economy had woken up and was getting on with its life.

Once out of the city and onto the network of country roads to the north, traffic soon thinned out. The farming world moved at a different pace. Within minutes, Jake could feel himself relaxing. They were on their way, low, forested hills in sight ahead of them. Their exit from Armona had gone better, far better, than he had feared it would.

CHAPTER FORTY-FIVE

It should have been good to be back in São Brás de Alportel. It had been home for several years. Jake liked both the town and his villa on the edge of it, and he and Magda had been living there together happily for some time. Even so, he didn't feel good about it now. It felt as if they were sacrificing something important to them both, and it went against his original intentions.

Their plan had changed en route. Thoughts of Pena had been jettisoned. An abandoned, and dilapidated, simple farm cottage in the depths of the countryside had ceased to appeal. It had not really been a viable option. Not with Yuri Bortsov for company. Jake had been coming to that conclusion himself even before Magda had begun to express similar doubts.

'Yuri may not like Pena,' Magda had pointed out in a worried tone as they drove north in what, until then, had been a happy, carefree manner.

'Like?' Jake said. 'What has like got to do with it? He doesn't like anything much anyway. He never has!'

Magda just shrugged.

Jake sighed. After another minute or two, he acknowledged reluctantly that she had come to the same opinion as he had himself.

Yuri seemed to value creature comforts highly. He had not defected to the West to live in a very substandard dacha, as he would undoubtedly have termed it, in the back of rural beyond. That had already been made crystal clear. Even idyllic Armona had been a severe disappointment to him. So there wasn't much doubt about how he would have regarded a ruined cottage in Pena.

'What might I not like about it?' Yuri asked.

'It is just a one-room cottage,' Magda told him.

'You go outside for water,' Jake added airily, 'and to go to the toilet.'

'Your bed will be made of solid wood,' Magda said, getting into the spirit of things.

'The floor is made of stone and dried mud,' Jake pointed out, 'and there is no electricity.'

'Or gas,' Magda contributed.

Yuri contemplated all this for a few moments before saying, 'You are making joke, yes?'

'No!' Magda said with a rueful chuckle. 'It's all true.'

'Don't worry, Yuri,' Jake said, compassion getting the better of him. 'We're not going there, after all. We'll go to São Brás instead, which is a very nice town with all modern facilities.'

Yuri sat back, shaking his head at the imbecility of the conversation, but clearly somewhat reassured by its conclusion.

'São Brás, though?' Magda said thoughtfully. 'Are you sure, Jake?'

He nodded. 'It's a better option than anywhere else I can think of.'

Better, perhaps, but not entirely good. Jake had accepted that they couldn't cope with Yuri in the cottage in Pena. No way in the world would he consent to being stuck there for an hour or two, never mind days on end. São Brás was a far better option, with its modern housing and facilities. Also, it was their home patch, and they knew their way around. Even so, he wasn't thrilled. He hated the idea of taking possible trouble so close to home, their hallowed ground.

* * *

144

Now, cruising along the Avenida, Jake's suspicious eyes were everywhere, scanning the pavement on both sides of the road in search of people who didn't belong. It wasn't rational, or even practical. He knew that, but he did it anyway. The Russians couldn't possibly have got here before them, because they hadn't known where they were going. Nor had he! So they couldn't possibly be here. Even so . . . !

The problem was that he couldn't bring himself to believe that they had really been shaken off. Not permanently. They had proved too many times that they were very adept at catching up, even when it had seemed as if the thread linking to them had been broken. He had no confidence that they couldn't do it again, even though they no longer had the tracker beacon to help them.

Jake's plan was to get out of sight and hunker down fast. And keep out of the way. Yuri, especially, would have to be invisible.

'We'll use your old flat,' he said to Magda. 'That all right with you?'

She looked at him with surprise.

'I would rather there than . . .' he added.

'All of us?'

He nodded. 'I know it's not very big, but it's only for a few more days now.'

She thought for a moment before giving her agreement. He knew she would feel the same way as him about their villa, just in case.

'You think they will follow us to São Brás?'

He shrugged. 'Who knows? Don't ask me how, but they might.'

* * *

The flat Magda had lived in before she and Jake hooked up was in a modern building six storeys high that was just off the Avenida. It was fortunate that Magda hadn't yet decided to sell her old home, given the current situation. A flat in the centre of town was ideal for them now. All they had to do was keep Yuri indoors for another couple of days. Then Henderson could have him — and as far as Jake was concerned, he was welcome to him!

They parked in the designated private parking space at the rear of the building and headed inside. If Yuri had expected something better, Jake noted, he was wisely keeping it to himself. Perhaps he hadn't. Perhaps he was just so tired and confused about everything that had happened to him lately that he no longer cared about anything very much at all. To be fair, that would be perfectly understandable after the last few weeks, let alone what he had been through before his so-called 'rescue'.

All that said, Magda's flat wasn't bad at all. It was just a very ordinary, modern, well-equipped little abode located in a surprisingly tranquil cul-de-sac off the main street. Perfect for their remaining time together. He and Magda could take turns shopping locally for groceries, but otherwise, they wouldn't need to leave the flat very much at all.

There was another, and very compelling, reason to use, or at least to visit Magda's flat. As soon as they had moved in and shut the door, Jake went to work with a screwdriver and removed a wall panel in the main bedroom. From the space behind it, he removed a Glock pistol and several boxes of bullets. Now there were no more international borders to cross, he was happy to risk carrying a weapon. Although the countdown was looming, he feared that it might still be needed.

CHAPTER FORTY-SIX

When Jake phoned him, Henderson confirmed that all was in order at his end. He had an exfiltration team ready to fly in and take Bortsov off Jake's hands in forty-eight hours' time.

'Not at the Faro international airport,' Jake said. 'I expect that to be heavily covered, and they'll be pretty desperate by now.'

'No, not Faro. A small military airport that is well protected by American as well as Portuguese personnel.'

That sounded better. The international airport at Faro was the main hub for the whole of the Algarve, and possibly even beyond. Trying to protect Yuri there would be a nightmare, and pretty much guaranteed to fail. A crowd scene or a well-positioned sniper could do the job equally well for the Russians. They would be spoilt for choice. A busy international airport was the last place he wanted to take his man after everything they had been through together.

Jake still believed the Russians would have preferred to abduct Yuri, but if that was no longer a realistic possibility, he couldn't see them being prepared to stand by and watch him be carried away by Giles Henderson, the CIA or anybody else. If necessary, the people who had chased them across the continent would probably be prepared to die in their attempt to prevent that. There would be no point going home if they failed.

Moving on to discuss where the exchange should take place, Jake put his foot down again when Henderson assumed it would be wherever Jake was currently holed up.

'Definitely not,' Jake said sharply. 'I'll bring him to a rendezvous we can agree nearer the time. That will be far safer. I don't want to risk someone else getting there before us because there's been a leak in London. So don't ask me where we are — and don't ask the boffins to find out either! I want to keep him safe until the handover.'

'Quite so,' Henderson said with apparent approval. 'Unfortunately, you're right to be so cautious. I've heard that General Oleg Blok has been brought back from retirement specifically to stop Bortsov's defection from happening.'

'Blok? Never heard of him.'

'No, I don't suppose you have. You had nothing to do with monitoring the trouble in the North Caucasus, did you?'

'Not a thing, thank God!'

'Well, you can count your blessings. Blok is very effective, and tough as they come. He'll try to bring this to an end any way he can. Be warned.'

'Duly noted.'

Jake repeated that he wanted to agree a location for the handover nearer the time. Then he ended the call.

Thinking about it afterwards, Jake felt he'd been well within his rights in not disclosing their current location to Henderson. Alongside the operational reasons of the line being potentially compromised, it wasn't just the villa or the flat he was thinking of. It was São Brás in general. He didn't want the Russians anywhere near the town. The exfiltration team could do their job elsewhere. Fortunately, Henderson had seemed to understand and had been prepared to go along with him on that.

* * *

Despite the circumstances, the tension and the constant need to be on guard, it was still a relief to be back in the town Jake had called home for the past few years. It was only a small, provincial town serving an ordinary rural area, but it had everything he needed and wanted. And more.

The sun-baked centre with its gentle traffic and white buildings, the newly planted avenue of trees and the well-cared-for beds of flowers and shrubs, it was good to see the town flourishing again. There were no big shops, and still fewer shopping centres, in São Brás, but so what? Shopping never had been a recreation activity for him. He could get most things he needed from the little family-owned shops that dominated the Avenida. These days there was also the internet if all else failed.

The first morning they were there, Jake went out early, leaving Magda and Yuri to have a leisurely breakfast together. He visited the market hall to buy fresh fish, vegetables and fruit. Bread, as well. And he went there first because the market hall was the social hub of the town in the mornings; it was where people gathered, as well as shopped for fresh food. They met friends and neighbours there, and they plugged into the networks distributing news and gossip. Jake wanted to test the atmosphere, to pick up anything out of the ordinary that might have happened lately.

He also went there because he couldn't shake off the worry that this wasn't over. Even here, of all places, he didn't feel safe. Nor did he feel Yuri was safe, not after everything that had happened in the past few weeks. It was still impossible for him to believe they were in the clear. If anything, now they were so close to the end of their time together, his fears were even greater.

He touched the cool metal of the Glock nestled in his waistband, but felt little in the way of reassurance. Even carrying a handgun at all times was scant protection, given what they were up against, but it was something. And until now, he hadn't even had that.

Yet, he was relieved to find life on the street seemed normal, and agreeably tranquil. That didn't mean he had no need to be anxious. It just meant he had no more reason to worry *yet*.

CHAPTER FORTY-SEVEN

In the afternoon, it was Magda's turn to venture out of the flat to look around. She would have liked to do a little shopping herself, but that wasn't possible. Afternoons were siesta time in São Brás. Virtually all the shops were closed. So instead, she contented herself with a gentle stroll that didn't quite count as exercise.

Yuri was confined to the great indoors. No way was he allowed out on the street, despite his half-hearted protestations. With so little time left of the operation, Jake was determined to keep him mothballed and out of sight until he was taken off their hands.

Fortunately, Yuri didn't seem to mind too much. He appeared happy to sit and think or do whatever it was that went on inside his head. Planning, fantasising, indulging himself in nostalgia, or regrets, even? Whatever. Usually he was in the bedroom he had been allocated, but that afternoon, he sat in the living room and mostly stared at the wall, to Jake's mounting irritation. Still, that was better than having him pestering to be allowed outside.

'Yuri,' Jake said after a while of watching him do, well, nothing. 'You really are a strange man. What are you thinking while you sit there staring at the wall?'

'I'm working on my book.'

'Working on . . . ?' Jake broke off with a chuckle. 'What book is that, Yuri?'

Looking puzzled for once, Bortsov stared at him. 'Didn't they tell you about it?'

Jake smiled and shook his head. Goodness, he thought! Yuri displaying a sense of humour? Well, it was very welcome, even if it had been a long time coming.

'They told me nothing, Yuri, next to nothing about you. It was all very hurried. They just wanted me to collect you and safeguard you for a month. There was certainly no mention of a book.'

Yuri looked disappointed. 'They are not really interested, are they?'

'I don't know.'

Jeez! he thought. What have we got here? What fantasy is this?

'What's the book about?'

'The battle.'

'Oh, I see. What battle is that?'

'The Battle of Kursk, of course.'

Jake stared for a moment and then shook his head. 'I don't understand. Kursk? Isn't that where something happened in World War Two?'

'Yes. That's what I'm talking about.'

'I still don't understand,' Jake said again.

'How could you? But I am from Kursk. It is my hometown.'

Ah! That rang a bell. Hadn't Henderson told him that?

'All my life,' Yuri continued, looking quite animated now, 'I have been interested in the famous battle there during the Great Patriotic War. One reason is that a great injustice was done during it to my grandfather.'

'Oh?'

'He was executed.'

'Oh?'

'Because his officer did not believe my grandfather's tank would not go anymore. Was broken. But he was wrong.'

Jake just shook his head, but Yuri wasn't finished.

'When I can, I work on my book about it, as I am doing now. But at home, I was allowed less and less time for it, and in the end, that became unacceptable to me. For that, as well as many other reasons, I had to leave.'

'I see.'

But he didn't. Cogs churned clumsily inside Jake's head and the fog shifted a little, but not by much.

'Yuri, are we talking about a big tank battle that occurred there in 1943 or '44?'

'Of course! It is my life's work.'

Jake managed not to laugh. 'And are you working on it now?' he asked carefully.

'Yes. Always.'

Dear God! Jake thought, feeling dizzy. He means it. The poor man must have cracked, mentally, psychologically. The stress has been too much for him.

Jake thought he would have to be careful now, or he might have a real problem on his hands. Henderson wouldn't thank him for that.

'I don't see you writing, Yuri,' he said gently. 'Are you sure? There's no pen and paper. No keyboard.'

'Of course not. It is impossible to have such things. They would never have allowed it. I write in my head, invisibly.'

Jake felt even more faint. 'And then what?' he managed to ask in a casual tone.

Yuri shrugged. 'I remember, of course.'

'Remember what?'

'What I have written.'

'Everything? It's all in your head?'

'Yes. I have written thirty-nine chapters so far.'

Jake nodded. Then he shut up, and the room became silent for minutes on end.

CHAPTER FORTY-EIGHT

In his head? Jake thought desperately. Is he round the twist? In fantasy land? Has he cracked?

Or do I believe him?

I do, actually, he decided. It might be crazy, but I do believe him.

Then the pieces of the puzzle began to fit together in a way they never had before. Not in all the miles they had travelled together, and amid all the dangers they had faced.

And he knew now where the secret information everybody seemed to want must be. No pellet. No microdot — or anything else. It was all in Yuri's head.

That was why all sides wanted a piece of him, and why the side that had once believed they owned him would never let him go. They simply couldn't. He really was a very special person.

'Yuri,' Jake said slowly, 'you have just made me realise how little I know about you. Next to nothing, in fact.'

'That is how it is — and how it has to be,' Yuri said gravely. 'But I did tell you I was very important, didn't I?'

'Yes, you did. And I had noticed that you have a very good memory.'

'That is true. I do.'

'And now you tell me you have a book in your head. Is that also really true?'

'Yes.'

'Can you remember other things?'

'Yes. Everything. My head is full.'

'What do you know about me, for instance? What have I told you, or have you learned, while we have been together?'

'Not so much.' Yuri frowned. 'You are very . . . guarded. Guarded? Is that correct?'

'It's the right word, certainly.'

'Well . . . Your birthday is on the first day of April. In your culture, that makes you a fool. I am sorry, Jake. Is that also correct?'

Jake nodded. 'Go on.'

'You have a cottage in somewhere called Northumberland. In England, I believe. It was burnt down by your enemies, but you have had it rebuilt, and now it is nearly finished. You also have a home in this town, São Brás. You live here with Magda. You used to be a spy, but now you are retired.'

Yuri looked puzzled for a moment before continuing. 'Even so, you have a boss. He is called Henderson, Sir Giles Henderson. He is in the British intelligence service, but I don't know which branch. Nor do I know how he can be your boss if you are retired. Explain, please?'

'It doesn't matter,' Jake said. 'Don't worry about it.'

Yuri then recited the truck's licence plate number with a self-deprecating shrug. 'Just little things like that,' he concluded.

Little things? Well, yes. That's what they were, on the whole, but they were also true. He couldn't recall divulging most of them. They must have just slipped out. But Yuri had them dead right. Amazing, really.

'That's enough, Yuri. I'm impressed. You really do have a good memory.'

Yuri shrugged. 'What I have said so far is very little. I know much, much more.'

'I believe you. I'm sure you do. You seem to have a photographic memory.'

'Perhaps. I don't know that term. But I do know that my memory is thought by experts to be special.'

'I bet! These would be Russian Intelligence service experts? In the employ of the GRU, perhaps?'

Yuri nodded.

'And you must know a lot about your country's intelligence work?'

'Much. Very much. Not everything, but a lot.'

'Thank you, Yuri. From what you have just told me, a lot of things make sense to me now. I just wish we had had this conversation earlier, much earlier.'

And he just wished Henderson had been more open with him. No wonder Mr Bortsov was so highly regarded.

'This will be why the Russians want you back? Because of your memory?'

'Yes.'

'And why the Americans also want you?'

'Yes. They made promises, but I think they lied.'

'What did they promise you?'

'That I would be able to work on my book in one of their great university libraries.'

'I see.'

What he could see was that they were unlikely to have much truck with that. They would have far more important things in mind for him.

'Thank you, Yuri. I understand much more now.'

'Yes,' Yuri said. 'I hoped you would.'

'One more thing,' Jake said with sudden inspiration. 'Does the name Oleg Blok mean anything at all to you? General Oleg Blok?'

'Yes. It does.'

Yuri stared into space for a few moments before saying, 'He is the one who recruited me for the GRU, and he is the person who made my life a misery and refused to allow me to leave. It was a great injustice.

'But, then,' he added after another pause, 'injustice runs in his family. They have a talent for it. I believe it is in their genes.'

'I see,' Jake said again, wondering what all that was about. 'What else can you tell me about this General Blok?'

'He retired last year.'

'I've been told he has returned to his old job.'

That caused Yuri's head to rotate fast. 'That will be because of me,' he said slowly.

'You think?'

'For sure.'

'Because?'

'Because he knows me very well. They will think he can find me and stop me leaving.'

Yuri looked troubled now, as if a door had been opened onto memories he would rather not have.

'He's not doing very well at the moment, is he?' Jake said with a smile. 'You've already left. What else can you tell me about him?'

'He is a very cruel man who had much success in helping to stop the rebellion in the North Caucasus. Many, many people were killed because of him, and his actions. Human life doesn't matter to him. He is . . . utterly ruthless.' Yuri concluded with a masterly use of the English language.

'What does—?' Jake began before spinning round and looking up as the door opened to reveal an agitated-looking Magda.

'Jake, I don't want to worry you,' she said, 'but we need to talk.'

'We certainly do. I've got a lot to tell you.'

CHAPTER FORTY-NINE

Yuri got up and walked out of the room purposefully.

'Where's he going now?' Jake asked wonderingly.

'To have a shower, perhaps?' Magda smiled. 'Or, more likely, to study the local maps on the bookshelf in his bedroom. He seems fascinated by them. Why — is there a problem?'

Jake shook his head. 'No. It gives me the chance to have a private word with you.'

'Oh?'

'I learned more about Yuri this afternoon, while you were out, than I had learned in the previous month. I believe I know now why he is so important to so many people — to so many countries, I should say.'

'I'm intrigued.'

'He's a pretty special sort of person, you know. I never realised that.'

'Well, he's autistic. I don't know if that makes him particularly special.'

'Autistic? What makes you think that?'

'Just how he is,' Magda said with a shrug. 'You know . . . How he thinks and talks, his lack of empathy, his social awkwardness, his egocentricity and tunnel vision, his . . . well, just everything about him!'

Jake shook his head. 'I never guessed. I never thought of autism, not that I know anything about it. He just seemed a selfish, difficult, oafish sort of fellow to me, until just now. When did you decide all that about him?'

'After about half an hour in his company,' Magda said with a smile. 'He reminds me of my cousin, Josef, actually. He's a professor at the Charles University in Prague. A very clever man.

'At first, like you, I just thought Yuri was a difficult, ungrateful sort of man who was too full of himself and had little regard for anyone else. But I soon realised there was a pattern, and . . . well, that he is what he is,' she finished with another shrug.

'Autistic?'

Magda nodded. 'But in itself, that doesn't make him anything special. It's being diagnosed with increasing frequency these days. Ultimately, we're all supposed to be on the autism spectrum, with varying levels of tendency in that direction. So, no, that aside, I have no idea why anyone thinks Yuri is important.'

Jake said with a wry smile, 'Well, I can help you there. Like your cousin, Yuri is a very clever man.'

'Well, I've come to realise that.'

'Part of it comes from him having a photographic memory.'

Magda stared at him for a moment and then nodded. 'Some autistic people do have very good memories. But go on!' she urged.

'He has total recall, seemingly, of just about anything he's ever seen or heard.'

'Really?'

'Apparently.'

Magda sat down heavily on a kitchen chair. 'Jesus, Maria!' she said in awe. 'Then he really is special. And he's an intelligence officer?'

Jake nodded.

'So the Russians can't afford to lose him, can they?'

'Not likely! And our side would give blood to get him.'

'Poor Yuri!'

Jake strode around the room while he marshalled his thoughts. Magda sat and waited as patiently as she could.

'First,' Jake resumed, 'there's the historical dimension. Yuri can't possibly know literally everything, of course, but what he does know about Russian Intelligence operations would probably fill the Library of Congress, or the British Museum. Although he's not very interested in that side of things, he admitted he knows a lot. And I'm sure he does.'

'That's one reason why your Mr Henderson regards him as important.'

'And why American agents died in their attempt to extract him.'

They digested that thought for a moment. Then Jake said, 'Then there's the current dimension.'

'What's that?'

'Well, we thought of inserted pellets and microdots, but there's a much easier and safer means of getting information across international borders, isn't there?'

'Just use someone with a photographic memory.'

Jake nodded. 'And show him the info you want to send, possibly to your agents in another country. Possibly details of financial arrangements. Or, maybe, listings of one kind or another — contacts, agents, blackmail material, etcetera, etcetera.'

'Phew!' Magda blew out her cheeks. 'This could be enormous.'

'Yes. And I think it probably is.'

'The implications for Russia and for the West scarcely bear thinking about.'

'That's true,' Jake conceded, 'but I'm more interested in the personal dimension.'

'What's that?'

'It seems obvious to me,' Jake said with a rueful smile and a shrug. 'The Russians have been trying everything they can to get their man back, and so far, they have failed. If they can't get him, I doubt they'll allow us or the Americans to have him. It will be Gotterdammerung all over again!'

'They will kill him, you mean?'

He nodded. 'Try to, at least. And they won't spare the people who they must know by now have been helping him, either. That's us,' he added unnecessarily.

They gazed long and hard at one another until Magda said, 'Your Mr Henderson needs to get the handover right, doesn't he? And soon.'

'Amen to that,' Jake said with conviction.

'The other thing I discovered this afternoon,' he added after a short pause, 'is what he's doing right now.'

'Nothing, isn't it?'

'That's what I thought. We're both wrong. He's writing a book.'

'Not that I've noticed,' Magda said with a smile.

'In his head.'

Magda laughed now. Then she stopped when he didn't join her. She looked at him quizzically for a moment and then said, 'You mean it, don't you?'

Jake nodded. 'Nothing on paper or on a computer device. He says that was too risky, and he wasn't allowed to do anything like that, anyway. It's in his head.'

'Do you believe that?'

'Strangely enough, yes. I do. I believe him. Thirty-nine chapters he says he's done so far. I asked him to tell me about Chapter Nineteen — a random choice, by the way — and after he'd recited about six pages of it, I told him to stop. That was enough.'

There was a long lull in the conversation at that point, each with much to consider.

'What's the book about?' Magda asked eventually.

'The Battle of Kursk, an enormous tank battle in the Second World War that lasted a week or more. It finished the Germans in Russia, I believe.'

Magda considered this new information. 'Is all this true, Jake?' she asked eventually.

'Yes. True, and real. It's his life's work. Yuri says he left Russia because they wouldn't leave him alone to work on it.'

'I'm finding all this a little difficult to comprehend.'

'Yeah. Me too.'

'So what does he expect to happen now?'

'He didn't really spell it out. But he seems to expect he will be installed in his own room on a university campus somewhere in America, and left to get on with his book, his life's work.'

'Harvard, perhaps? Or one of those little places in California?'

'Davis, perhaps?' Jake nodded, but with a wry smile he added, 'I assume Sir Giles Henderson has a rather different idea.'

CHAPTER FIFTY

'Now, let me tell you about my afternoon,' Magda said. She didn't wait for a response. 'There were men speaking in Russian. Three of them, in that café in the market hall.'

Jake ran his hand over his brow, concerned. 'That doesn't sound good. Could you hear what they were saying?'

Magda shook her head. 'Just the odd few words. I could tell they were not on holiday.'

Jake grimaced.

'It was very noisy in there, as usual,' Magda continued, 'and I didn't want to move any nearer in case they thought me suspicious. What I heard was just when I went up to the counter to pay.'

'Bloody hell!' Jake said with a sigh. 'It sounds like they may have caught up with us again.'

He was anguished but not really surprised. All along, he had suspected and feared this might happen. It was no good wondering how they had done it, either.

They might still be innocent tourists, he supposed. That was possible, if unlikely. He had never seen or heard of any Russian holidaymakers coming to São Brás, but that didn't mean it couldn't happen. It wasn't a tourist town, but a few people with historical interests seemed to find their way here to look at the former bishop's palace and the cork museum. Not many, admittedly, but some.

Much more likely, though, was that the men Magda had noticed had come for Yuri, probably to wipe him off the face of the earth if they couldn't abduct him and take him back to Moscow.

Yuri had wandered back into the room while they were talking and had heard what Magda had had to say about the Russians. Jake asked him for his opinion.

'It is them,' he said flatly. 'No Russian people would come here for a holiday. There is no beach, and no big hotels. Where would they drink — and get drunk?'

Jake smiled. 'Jokes are good, Yuri. Keep it up!'

'No joke, Jake. I tell the truth. That is what Russian men like doing on holiday.'

'Just like us Brits, eh?' Jake smiled again, but he knew it had been wrong of him to suspect Yuri of telling a joke. It just wasn't in his nature, unfortunately. He was telling the truth, as he saw it.

'I agree with Yuri, Jake,' Magda said. 'I believe they are here for him, and probably for us too.'

That was much the same as Jake thought. 'Well,' he said, glancing at his watch, 'we just have to keep our heads down for another twenty-four hours. Then Yuri is out of here, off to somewhere suitably idyllic, and we'll be able to get on with our lives.'

Or not, he thought, being realistic.

* * *

Yuri had a question about something else. Could he have a phone?

'What for? What do you want a phone for?' Jake asked.

'I need to do some research.'

'Research? No phone calls, Yuri, remember?'

Yuri looked as if he felt slighted that Jake had questioned his memory.

163

Still, Jake hesitated.

Magda nudged him. 'Jake? That's OK, isn't it?'

Reluctantly, Jake sighed and nodded. He brought out a phone from his jacket pocket and handed it over.

'Remember, Yuri, no chatting on the phone! All right?'

'Yes, Jake,' Yuri said over his shoulder as he walked away. 'I mean no.'

Jake stared after him, wondering if he was missing something here. What did he want a phone for?

'It's to do some research for his book,' Magda said. 'The poor man has to do something to occupy his mind while we sit it out here.'

'I suppose so.'

Jake nodded and tried to dismiss his lingering doubts.

CHAPTER FIFTY-ONE

It was shortly before two in the morning, in the cool, small hours. Jake wasn't asleep. He was just lying there, resting, but too uneasy to sleep. The windows in the bedroom were open. He heard the quiet throb of an approaching vehicle. The vehicle slowed down and came to a gentle halt. The throbbing ceased. That was enough to get him out of bed.

He reached the window and carefully edged the curtain slightly aside. He was in time to see the interior lights of a car fade and die. In the light cast by one of the few street lamps still on, he saw several figures emerge from the vehicle and huddle together for a moment.

'Get up!' he whispered urgently to Magda, who he had heard stirring.

'Is it them?' she asked, instantly awake.

'Looks like it.' He grimaced. 'We'd better get out.'

Waking Yuri and getting him moving was more difficult.

'What is it?' he demanded petulantly.

'Get up, Yuri! We have to go.'

'Now?'

'Now,' Jake confirmed. 'The Russians are here.'

He didn't waste time wondering how it had happened. He just knew they had to get out before the door was smashed open and they came in with guns blazing. Once again, they had to run to stay ahead of the chasing pack. If they could do that for another day or so, it would be over at long last. If they couldn't do that, it would still be over — but so would they be.

As in the holiday cottage on Armona, emergency back-packs were waiting by the front door, a precaution that Jake had once again insisted on.

'Ready?' he asked a minute or two later.

Yuri, still zipping up his trousers, nodded. Magda was already waiting by the front door.

'Let's go,' Jake said, scooping up his backpack and heading for the exit.

* * *

They had been quick, but not quick enough.

Opening the door revealed the muffled sound of people making their careful way up the concrete stairwell. Trying to be quiet but failing in what was essentially an echo chamber.

'Get the lift!' he whispered to Magda. Then he turned and grabbed the two long-handled brooms kept in the small cupboard next to the front door of their flat.

At the top of the stairwell, a pair of swing doors gave access to their landing. They were supposed to be kept closed, for fire safety reasons, but they were wedged open now. They usually were in the warmer months, to improve the ventilation of the building.

Jake kicked the wedges away, closed the doors and threaded both brooms through the twin steel grab handles. The brooms were made of tough timber and would hold for a while, quite possibly for longer than the doors themselves.

The lift arrived. Jake ushered the others inside as a clamour began in the stairwell beyond the jammed doors, all attempts to maintain silence abandoned. He pressed buttons. The lift began to descend, but only for two floors. Then it stopped. Jake urged Magda and Yuri out. Before following them, he fixed the lift and sent it off on a journey to the twelfth floor, the top of the building. They needed every second they could win.

Magda raised an eyebrow, with a *what-now?* expression on her face.

'The empty flat,' he whispered, brushing past her.

All the flats in the block had a standard lock fitted to the front door. It was a simple mechanism and long ago Jake had worked out how to defeat it with a plastic card. In seconds, he had the door to the empty flat open. He ushered the others inside and closed the door quietly after them.

'They will find us here,' Bortsov said with resignation, rediscovering the standard attitude he hadn't used for a while.

'No, they won't,' Jake assured him. 'We're not staying. And you can stop that defeatism right now!'

Bortsov shrugged but said no more.

'Jake?' Magda said, also sounding worried.

'It's OK,' he assured her. 'We're leaving.'

The flat they had entered was on the first floor. The big living-room window looked out onto the parking area at the rear of the building, and the back of the buildings in the next street. Not much of a view, but Jake had identified it as a potential escape route if the need arose. Now it had.

Preparing an exit strategy in advance of needing one was something he hadn't stopped doing since leaving the service that had drilled the practice into him. There was a small balcony outside the living-room window of the flat. Immediately below that was the flat roof of an extension that had been built on to the ground-floor utility complex that served the whole building. A fixed ladder fitted for maintenance purposes connected the balcony to the flat roof below.

Jake opened the window on to the balcony and led the way to the ladder.

'Ah!' Magda said, understanding at last.

He motioned to her and she climbed over the balcony wall and began the descent. Yuri responded to Jake's urging and followed her down the ladder, albeit hesitantly. Jake closed the window and slid after him.

From the flat roof, they scrambled and jumped to the ground. Jake had a quick look around. There was no one in sight and nothing to suggest anyone had seen them. They hurried to the truck — Jake had taken to parking it on the next street, where the early-morning vans and trucks that delivered to the market hall parked, hiding it in plain sight.

Already there were people scurrying around the market, unloading fish, shovelling ice, bringing in new-dug potatoes and baking bread. They were far too busy to take notice of three extra bodies, Jake thought with relief as he climbed into the truck after the others.

CHAPTER FIFTY-TWO

'Where to now?' Magda asked as they left the lights of São Brás behind.

'You know as well as I do,' Jake said. 'There's only one place we can go.'

'Yes, I suppose so,' she said wearily.

They drove on into the blackness. No street lights out here, on the N2. No traffic either, not during the night. Even farmers and foresters wouldn't be out before daylight came. This way led into the wilderness, the wild country where few people lived and not many even visited.

The three of them were wedged onto the wide seat at the front of the truck. It was uncomfortable, noisy and hot, but none of them minded. They had made it. They had escaped! For now.

Jake was actually exhilarated to have got away from the flat so cleanly and easily. The adrenaline was still pumping half an hour later. He just hoped it kept going all through the new day. That was all they needed: one more day. Then they would be out and done. Yuri would be safe. And so would they — he hoped!

'Where do we go?' Yuri asked after a little while. 'I am tired.'

'You're tired?' Jake exclaimed. 'You're lucky you're not dead!'

It took a sharp dig in the ribs from Magda to quieten Jake's indignation. 'Jake!' she admonished, just in case he hadn't got the message.

'I know, I know,' he said ruefully. 'Sorry, Yuri!'

She was right, he thought with a grimace. When would he ever learn? Yuri had just said he was tired. That was all. It was perfectly understandable. He hadn't been complaining. Not this time. Just a statement of fact.

All the same . . . Relief, gratitude and everything else he ought to be feeling right now didn't come into it. He was tired, for God's sake! Statement of fact.

'We are going to a place we know in the hills,' Magda told Yuri patiently. 'It's a very quiet little village, and we will stay in an isolated cottage on the hillside that is even quieter. No one knows of it, and no one will bother us there.'

'What is the name of this place?' Bortsov asked, sounding suspicious.

It was Magda's turn to be jabbed in the ribs. If she told him the name of the place, he would undoubtedly remember all the disadvantages they had told him about it. And no doubt raise extra objections they didn't need to hear.

Besides, Jake had thought of something else, something that made him think there was no point taking unnecessary risks. 'It doesn't have a name,' he said. 'It's a place with no name: *Innominate*.'

'That is Latin,' Yuri pointed out.

'It is. You're right.'

'So it does have a name.'

'Right again. *Innominate*.'

A few minutes later, Magda whispered to Jake, 'That hurt. My ribs are sore now. Did you have to jab me so hard? Why was that necessary?'

'Everything has a reason, my dear. Inspiration struck. That is all I want to tell you right now.'

'Humph.'

* * *

They drove on, and on. Jake was thinking about how the Russians had managed to home in on them again, and wondering yet again how they had managed to do it. São Brás should have been beyond their reach, but it hadn't been. After a day or two's delay, they had found them once more, just as they had in Armona and everywhere else on this long, forever journey. Maybe Pena wouldn't be a problem for them either, even though for reasons hard to justify he had stopped Magda uttering the name aloud.

But how the hell had they done it?

He wrestled with that question for a while. Then one possibility struck him. Damn! Of course. Perhaps, anyway. Maybe.

He pulled off the road and stopped, keeping the engine running.

'Yuri, we need to get rid of your passport. Perhaps it really does have a microdot, which could be how they have been able to track us.'

'No!' Yuri came to life with a snap. 'Not my passport. I need it.'

'No, you don't. Be logical. I know you're good at it. If we're not successful at escaping, we'll probably all be dead. Magda and I will be, anyway. If we are successful, you'll be given a new identity — and a new passport. So you really don't need the one you've got, do you?'

'It's mine,' Yuri said sullenly. 'It's all I have from the life I left behind.'

'But you don't need it, do you?' Jake said firmly. 'And it may be putting us all in danger.'

Yuri shut up and stared unseeing into the blackness all around them.

Jake waited.

There was no further discussion until Magda said, 'Would it help, Yuri, if we give up our passports too?'

'No way—' Jake began.

'We don't need them either,' Magda pointed out reasonably. 'As you yourself said, Jake, either we will no longer be alive to use them or we will be given new passports. Especially me,' she added a moment later. 'Hopefully, one with my real name on it.'

That made Jake smile, if reluctantly. 'Will it be any better than the one you got from Mr Phan in Czechia?'

'I don't know. But it will be a proper British passport, won't it? Not one from Petrovice — or even Brussels!'

'Ah! That's true. I hadn't thought of that. A blue one, too. My favourite colour.'

'All right,' Yuri said, perhaps tiring of a conversation he didn't understand. 'You can have my passport, Jake, if you give up yours as well. We will give them to Magda.'

'Don't trust me, eh?' Jake said with a grin.

Jake dug into his jacket pocket and handed his passport to Magda. Yuri followed suit. Then Magda extracted her own passport and got out of the truck with all three documents, which she had put in a plastic bag.

'Done,' she said a minute or two later, when she reappeared. 'Now we are all stateless persons. But if we do wish to reclaim them, I know where they are. They will be safe.'

'I want an American passport, if I can't have my old one,' Yuri said gruffly. 'I don't want a blue one.'

'And I am sure that whoever is president of the United States, when he gets to hear of your sacrifice, will give you one,' Magda told him.

'Yes, I believe he will,' Yuri said.

He nodded then, satisfied that his rights and preferences would be honoured.

Jake smiled, kept quiet and got the truck moving again.

'So, go on then. Why did you dig me in the ribs back there?' Magda asked again a few minutes later. '*Innominate*, indeed!'

'Because I didn't want the true name mentioned.'

'I gathered that, but why?'

'Well, first, I didn't want to stir up things that had already been said. Problems and disadvantages.'

'Was there also another reason?'

Jake glanced across the seat at Yuri, who seemed to have gone to sleep.

'Yes,' he admitted. 'Apart from the passport, the only other explanation I can imagine for them being able to track us is that they fiddled with his brain.'

'Who's brain? Yuri's, you mean?'

Jake nodded.

'Oh, Jake! In what way?'

'I don't know. Perhaps by inserting a locator in it, or else they've come up with some other way of receiving automatic transmissions from it. I don't know! Call it superstition, if you like. I just didn't want to risk them somehow hearing the name mentioned.'

'That's all a bit far-fetched, isn't it?'

'It is. Absolutely. But if you can think of another explanation, be sure to let me know. It may save our lives!'

CHAPTER FIFTY-THREE

Daylight was spreading as they drove into Pena, the world starting to recover from darkness and sleep. A horse watched them. Sheep on their feet in a paddock ignored them, continuing to nibble at whatever they could find on ground left bare by their relentless foraging. An elderly woman, all in black, peered out at them from her shadowed doorway.

'Keep going,' Magda said. 'We're not there yet.'

On the other side of the small huddle of houses and rural buildings, she directed Jake to turn up a steep, rough track. He changed down, and down again, and began to climb through clouds of gravel and dust.

When they came to it, the cottage was exactly as he had expected: just another abandoned farmstead, like the one they had used the previous year. Once, a family would have lived here on what they grew and raised on their land, but not now, not anymore. The vegetable garden was overgrown by shrubs and young trees. The little fields beyond were stony wastelands hosting a meagre scattering of thorny, spiky plants well suited to the desert-like conditions.

Livestock pens and hutches, paddocks and barns, were all empty and dilapidated. The olive grove was still there, though, still centuries from maturity, and the durable cork oak trees stood silent and majestic. It would take more than a few decades of neglect to bring their lives to an end.

'This another of Kunda's properties?' Jake asked, referring to Magda's onetime boss in the Prague criminal underworld.

She nodded. 'Pavel will still own it — you don't let go of property once you have obtained it. He won't have been here for a long time, though.'

'If ever?'

'If ever,' she agreed. 'It was an investment, somewhere to deposit money where it couldn't be stolen, taxed or lost.'

Jake wondered if Kunda had envisaged building a summer residence here, but seemed unlikely. Living — even staying — somewhere like this probably wouldn't work for a city man like him. He would be bored to death.

They parked in front of the house, a white-painted stone structure that looked as if it had been there for ever, and now was gently melding into the rocky hillside. Magda got out of the truck.

Yuri woke up at that point. He glanced out of the window and said, as if out of habit, 'It is not much, this place, I think.'

'You're right,' Jake agreed. 'But hopefully it will serve us until tomorrow.'

'Where is Magda?'

'She has gone to get the key.'

'Why would anyone bother to lock a ruin?'

'Why, indeed?'

Jake knew what the cottage would be like on the inside. It would be hard for trespassers or vandals to spoil, short of setting fire to it. Just like the one they had used the previous year, it would be a one-roomed and very basic dwelling devoid of electricity, gas, internet coverage and everything else cherished by metropolitans and sophisticates like themselves — Yuri, especially!

'It won't have running water,' he said conversationally. 'That will be outside, like the toilet — although that may just be a hole in the ground.'

'The water is outside?' Bortsov said, shaking his head. 'I didn't know it could be like this in the West.'

'You've not been before?'

'No, never. I was too important to be allowed to leave Russia.'

'You have a lot to learn, then.'

Jake smiled and got out of the truck.

'Find it?' he called to Magda, who had reappeared from behind the building.

'Yes. It was there. Always the keys are in the same place with these houses.'

'You would think the criminals would know that.'

'There are no criminals, Jake, not here. They live in the cities, where there are things to steal.'

True enough, Jake thought ruefully. Slim pickings here.

Magda mounted the steps to the front door and used the key to open it. A smell of mould and decay wafted out immediately. Jake winced and wondered if they wouldn't be better off staying in the truck, but he followed Magda inside dutifully. At least they could lie down and stretch out here, if nothing else.

He had brought a torch from the truck, but by the time he got inside Magda had already located a candle and lit it with the old Zippo she always carried with her. Now, she turned to an oil lamp hanging from the ceiling.

'You've been here before,' Jake said with a chuckle.

'Oh, yes. Bring Yuri inside, while I sort out the lamp.'

* * *

Jake got a reluctant Yuri installed indoors. Then he hunted around outside, looking for a spot where he would have signal coverage for his mobile. That took some doing. In the end, he had to go a little way up the hillside to get a couple of bars.

Henderson answered his call promptly. 'Yes?'

'I need to sort out arrangements for the handover. The month is up today, remember?'

'Of course. The arrangements are in hand. Tell me, are you still having difficulty with our friends?'

'Very much so. They came for us again in the middle of the night. We managed to get out in time and move on.'

Henderson tutted and said, 'It's down to General Blok, I'm afraid. He's back in charge and seems to be giving it everything he's got. My understanding is that he has some sort of deal with the president. If he makes a success of this operation, he'll be a very wealthy man — and he may be back in post for good.'

'Which you wouldn't want to see happen?'

'Good heavens, no! He's far too dangerous an adversary.'

'Well, I don't know what the hell's going on, or how they're tracking us, but you've got to come and take this man off my hands now. I'm worn out, and I'm not the only one. If he's going to be any good to you, you need to get him away from here — and fast!'

'I do see that. And I quite agree — absolutely. Later today, if that's OK with you?'

'Yeah. The sooner, the better.'

'As for the location of the handover, there are two possibilities. One is that we come to you; the other is that you come to us. Which do you prefer? How safe do you feel where you are now?'

Jake gave a hollow laugh. 'I don't feel safe at all — anywhere! Nowhere feels safe now. Having said that, we're just not up to going any further. We're exhausted. Running on empty.'

'We'll come to you, in that case. Give me your coordinates.'

'You'd better keep them to yourself,' Jake said with feeling. 'I'll know who to blame if this goes wrong yet again.'

'I'm waiting, Jake,' Henderson said patiently, ignoring the slight.

Jake read out the coordinates from his phone.

'Is that a town or a village?'

'Neither. It's just outside a hamlet called Pena. We're in a cottage my partner has access to. How and when can we expect you?'

177

'Watch your phone for updates, Jake. But pick up will be at five this afternoon.'

'You hope!'

'Not hope, Jake. Intend. I intend.'

CHAPTER FIFTY-FOUR

'Five this afternoon, he said.'

Magda nodded and looked thoughtful. 'How will it work, Jake? Where do we need to get to?'

'Nowhere. We just stay here.'

'They will come here for Yuri?'

'Yes. An exfiltration team. They'll be experienced at that sort of thing.'

'How many people will be in the team?'

He shrugged. 'I don't know. Enough, I hope. Anyway, it's better than us going to the airport to meet them. I wasn't looking forward to that. It's too public, too risky.'

Yuri, who had been listening to what was being said, spoke up. 'The British won't send enough men,' he said. 'They never do. The Americans would send . . . well, the Seventh Fleet, for someone like me.'

Jake laughed. Yuri seemed to be cheering up, he thought with approval.

'Nuclear submarines, as well?' he suggested. 'Like they did when you were in Slovakia?'

Yuri frowned. That wasn't funny. He didn't like to think of what had happened back there.

Magda winced at the exchange and glowered at Jake, signalling that he shouldn't rile Yuri with sarcasm.

Jake went back outside, chastened. All the same, he feared Yuri might well be right in these cost-straitened times. He would just have to hope the extraction team came mob-handed. The Russians certainly would if they found out where Yuri was.

* * *

There were fine views from up here. Jake stood at the edge of the old kitchen garden and looked out over a great swathe of little-populated countryside. Immediately in front of him, the hillside sloped down and away into the distance, across miles and miles of land that had been farmed since the dawn of time but looked little like English farmland. The farms here were mostly smallholdings producing vegetables and fruit, nuts and timber. And olives, of course, and bark from the cork oak trees. Many would have a cow or two, goats, a few sheep perhaps, and a handful of chickens and other fowl, but not livestock on a scale a Northern European farmer would identify with.

Now, though, there were many abandoned farmsteads. Making a living from the land was so hard, and the attraction of the hospitality industry in the coastal resorts so alluring, especially to the young. The elderly stayed, of course, stayed till the very end, but there were not so many of them left now. The world had moved on without them.

Jake turned and gazed at the towering hillside behind him, the great mass of craggy limestone known as Rocha da Pena. Ancient and, as seen from here, rugged and bare. But the flat top, a mile or two long, was cloaked with vegetation and would once have been farmed too, judging by the Iron Age wall that he knew had been built near one end to defend it. Now it was home to wild boar and a range of other mammals, as well as reptiles, birds and an infinite variety of insects.

If the Russians found them here, Jake surmised, turning to look to his front again, they would come from the south. They would come along the road, the only road, along the valley from Salir. Then they would have to take the rough track from the foot of the hillside, just as they had done themselves. There was no other way. That's if they did come, of course. Right now, it seemed improbable that they would, but Jake didn't rule it out. Why would he? The Russians had found them everywhere else they had been.

He didn't know in detail what Henderson intended. All he could do was assume that Henderson's exfiltration team would be up to the job. They would certainly have been made aware of the risks and the dangers. Henderson would surely have seen to that. At least, Jake thought with a frown, he certainly hoped he had.

As for himself, there wasn't much more he could do now. Waiting was about the only thing on his agenda. Eight hours to go, he thought with a glance at his watch. Eight more hours to survive, and to avoid having to spend a night in that damned hovel behind him.

CHAPTER FIFTY-FIVE

They arrived in the early afternoon, at what could have been the height of siesta time. The whole world might have been asleep had it not been for the constant drone and whirring of a billion, billion insects.

In his lookout position on the hillside, Jake froze for a moment. Then he hurriedly wiped his eyes with the back of his hand to clear them before squinting hard through the shimmering waves of heat rising from the thin scatter of lavender and gorse, thyme and eucalyptus, and the bare ground in between. He confirmed his first impression. The Russians were here.

Two big four-by-fours. Toyotas, they looked like. Land Cruisers. They had pulled into the small parking area next to the information board at the foot of the hill. Men spilled out of them. Jake counted six before he gave up and called over his shoulder to alert the others.

Magda pushed through the shrubs to reach his side. Pulling back to let her see for herself, he said, 'Definitely not the exfiltration team.'

'No,' she said after a quick glance. 'They're Russians.'

Jake watched for a few more moments as the men deployed at the bottom of the hill and made their preparations. Then he got to his feet.

'Come on,' he snapped. 'We'd better get moving.'

There was no chance of avoiding detection by staying in the only building standing on this part of the hillside. It would be the first place searched. So they were to be spared the ordeal of spending any more time in the derelict cottage, listening to Yuri complaining about it. There was always something to be grateful for.

While Magda got their emergency packs from the truck, Jake stayed and watched as the Russians gathered to receive their battle orders. The leader held what looked like an iPad, which he consulted before looking up to give his men their instructions. He seemed to have a good idea of where he wanted them to go. Straight up! That would cover it more than adequately, Jake felt.

'That is not Colonel Kozlov,' Yuri said over Jake's shoulder.

'Oh?'

'He replaced, or succeeded, General Blok. But that is Sergeant—'

Jake cut him off. There wasn't time for it. 'All right!' he said. 'I believe you.'

'He is here because I am important,' Yuri said with apparent satisfaction.

'All right, Yuri,' Jake said with a grin. 'I am ready now to accept that you are important.'

'Thank you, Jake.'

Jake scrambled to his feet. 'Let's go,' he snapped.

The man could drive you mad at times, Jake thought, shaking his head. There was no harm in him, though, and he knew now why Yuri was regarded as such a valuable asset. Not as a human being, though. More as a portable intelligence archive. Yet, despite that, in a sense he was a throwback to a simpler age, one where it was people and not technology that counted.

* * *

Sweating with more than the heat now, Jake gave Henderson a quick call as the others made final preparations.

'If your team can't get here in force in the next five minutes,' he said brusquely, 'they needn't bother. The Russians have arrived, and they're mob-handed. We're about to move out across the hillside. We've got to move!'

'How many men have they got?'

'Maybe a dozen. I don't know exactly.'

'That many?' Henderson said with surprise.

'They've been putting a lot into this all along. I've tried to tell you that. Why would they stop now? The man they want keeps telling me how important he is, and by now I'm ready to believe him.'

'Quite. Just so.'

Following a brief pause, Henderson said, 'It looks like rocky country where you are, Jake. Just find somewhere to hide. And keep your phone on!'

Jake wondered if Henderson was looking at a map or an aerial photograph. Or possibly a live scan from a satellite.

'There's no sign of the exfiltration team,' Jake pointed out. 'I have to tell you we really need them — or somebody! — right now. We're desperate.'

'Do what I said, Jake. Hide. Just do it!'

'Then what?'

'We'll find you.'

'How?'

But Henderson had ended the call, and it really was time to go. The only thing he knew with any certainty was that they couldn't stand still. They had to move.

He turned, nodded to the others and set off to lead the way along a possible escape route he had picked out several hours earlier. Not a path, exactly. Far from it. But it had looked as if it might be doable.

'It is impossible,' Yuri protested as they began clambering over boulders.

'No, it isn't! Staying here is what's impossible.'

'You should just give me up. That will be best. I will probably survive.'

'You might, being such an important person. But what about us?'

'It is hopeless, Jake. There is no point going on. They always win.'

'For crissake, shut the fuck up! I'm warning you, Yuri. I'm going to get really annoyed if you start this again.'

'It is the truth,' Yuri said, undaunted. 'It is what I have always said.'

'Damn right you have! And I'm sick of hearing it. But I'm not giving you up, Yuri. You can forget that. I might have done a month ago, but not now, not after everything we've been through to get this far.'

Yuri just shrugged. At least, he's moving, Jake thought, which means he doesn't really want to give up either. He's just scared, perhaps close to being overwhelmed. Well, join the club, old cock! You're not the only one, he thought grimly.

'Where are we going?' Magda wanted to know.

'There's another cottage on this hill. Remember?'

'It burned down, Jake. Surely you haven't forgotten?'

'I don't mean that one.'

Magda was quiet for a moment. Then she said, 'Oh! Those old people's house? The ones that helped us last year?'

Jake nodded.

'We can't put them in danger again!'

'We're not going to. They aren't there anymore.'

'What do you mean?'

'They've gone. I looked, and their farm is deserted, abandoned.'

'Oh, no!'

'It doesn't look as if anything very terrible happened. They've just upped sticks and left. Probably gone into the town. Retired.'

'Yes, probably. It would be better for them there.'

Jake gave a helping hand to Yuri, who was struggling to keep up. While he did so, his mind went racing through the gears, considering options. There weren't many. The situation was more desperate by the minute. They were nearly out of time.

He had an inkling of what Henderson had in mind. Escape was still possible. But the time they had left was minutes now. Something had to happen very, very soon. Or . . .

Sod that! No way was he giving up. He would fight to the end, like he always had.

CHAPTER FIFTY-SIX

If ever there had been a path along the contour they were attempting to follow, it had been a very long time ago. Perhaps in the Iron Age, or even the Stone Age, Jake thought, as they threaded their way as fast as they could between jagged rocks and through tangles of vicious thorn. Not since.

For Jake, the best thing about the route they were taking was that it was hidden from anyone watching from below. A bulge in the steeply sloping hillside meant that they were out of sight of the Russians. He had factored that in when working it out as a possible escape route.

It was hard work and slow going, but they were moving, making progress, and doing the best they could. Even Yuri had buckled down to it, his habitual pessimism and dire predictions set aside. Not forgotten, though, Jake thought with a malicious grin. Never that, knowing him! He's just knackered. We all are.

Then another thought struck him like a shaft of light through a darkening sky. Of course, that was why Yuri usually kept it up, that infuriating flow of negativity. It was his coping strategy. How very bloody Russian! Expect the worst, the very worst, and you will never be disappointed. Anything less, any little thing at all, will be a victory to be savoured.

* * *

'I think we're being followed,' Magda said, breaking into Jake's thoughts.

What? Gasping for breath, he paused to listen, motioning to Yuri to be still too. Now he could hear something. The occasional sound of boots slipping and slithering on gravel, scraping on rock. Small avalanches of dislodged stones. Not close, but still ominous. Magda was right. The Russians were on their trail.

How many men were coming? Not all of them. That was for sure. Maybe just a couple of wing men at the edge of the search party moving up the hillside, checking out possibilities. The focus would still be on the cottage, and the truck alongside it. That was where they would expect to find them.

Jake really didn't think they could have been spotted. Men coming this way would just be part of covering all the options. No manpower shortage, after all. They had men to spare, he thought grimly.

As for themselves, the moment of truth had finally come. It was time now for him to do more than just run. They had been doing that for far too long. He and Magda might have been able to stay ahead of the chasing pack a bit longer, but not with Yuri in tow.

The little Russian was doing very well. Jake couldn't fault him or complain about his performance right now, but Yuri was no outdoors man. He was no fitter or more capable in country like this than anyone else would be who spent their life in a library or in front of a computer screen. The men following them were not like that. They would be tough, experienced field operatives, capable of going all day while killing and doing anything else required of them.

It was time to try to do something about the capability gap. They couldn't wait any longer for Henderson's people. The promised exfiltration team were not even on the battlefield. They seemed more like a myth than a reality. Jake knew it was down to him alone now. He had to do something soon, very soon, or give up and be shot dead on the spot.

He told Magda to press on with Yuri. She knew what that meant and looked gravely worried. But she knew what he had to do as well as he did himself. Jake had to hold them up. Somehow. So she nodded and kissed him on the cheek. Then she turned to urge Yuri onward.

Jake didn't watch them go. He turned back and focused on what he had to do himself.

A big rock they had just passed offered a possible vantage point. He swarmed up it and settled behind a thorny shrub on the top. He didn't have to wait long. Two or three minutes only. He had almost left it too late. Then they appeared.

There were two of them. Lean, hard men, moving easily and fast. His heart sank a little. He had seen their type before. *Spetsnaz*. Russian special forces. Fit, trained and tough. Used to rough terrain in hostile environments, experienced and always up for a fight.

They seemed confident they were on to something. Confident, too, about what the outcome would be. They were carrying the standard-issue submachine guns used by their service, and Jake had no doubt at all that they were ready to use them.

He made a quick assessment. In another two or three minutes, they would catch up. And then it would all be over. Wipeout for himself and Magda. Quite possibly for Yuri, too, despite his belief to the contrary.

Jake knew what he had to do. It was a classic situation: them or us, all over again.

CHAPTER FIFTY-SEVEN

With two submachine guns coming his way, the odds were not good. The firepower gap had to be reduced. The only way to do it was by striking first and hard.

Yet against the normal self-preservation instinct, he had to let them come closer first. A pistol wasn't much good at any sort of real distance. Tense, he focused. The two men drew steadily closer. Moving fast and eagerly; like hounds in full flow, they had the scent. They had seen signs on the ground. They knew they were on the right trail and close.

He could see their faces now. It didn't help. The opposite, in fact. These were not the men he had seen in the hotel in Budva all that time ago. These were not forensic investigators or cops at home on city streets. These were men used to battlefields in hard country. They were the perfect choice for the job at hand.

When they were only a couple of yards short of his position, Jake raised the Glock and fired three times at the second of the two men. At least one of the shots hit the target. The man grunted, staggered and lurched sideways before collapsing to the ground.

Jake didn't wait to see more. He tossed a big stone behind the men and dropped to the ground as bullets raked that area and then the bushes that had been his shelter.

The vanishingly small advantage of surprise had gone now. He poked the Glock round the corner of the rock and fired more shots blind before risking taking a look. The lead Russian had just finished firing at the place where the stone Jake had thrown had landed. Now he was scrambling to check on his partner. He sensed movement behind him and swung back round just as Jake fired two shots at him. A wild burst from his submachine gun created a cloud of dust, and chunks of rock cascaded onto Jake.

Instinct kicked in. Jake had to move fast and aggressively or he was done for. It wasn't possible to fight defensively with a handgun when your opponent was coming at you, firing hundreds of rounds a second.

Forlorn hope! He took two more blind shots and then hurled himself forward. Hitting the ground and rolling, he swung his gun arm round to shoot again. But he couldn't see a target. There was no target! Where the hell was he?

Jake rose onto his knees, pistol ready, searching for the man with the submachine gun. It took a second or two before he located him through the dust storm that had been created. He was face down in the dirt, his weapon a yard or two away from him.

Jake scrambled to his feet and scooped up the fallen gun. Then he gave the body a kick, checking that the man really was dead, and went looking for his colleague.

He found him close by, still alive but obviously badly wounded. He had managed to crawl out of the way under a spiky thornbush. He was still nursing his submachine gun, and still a danger. Without hesitation, Jake shot him in the head with the Glock, regretting only the necessity of using one more of the few rounds he had left for it.

Now he had two submachine guns. He considered for a moment before tossing one away as an unnecessary encumbrance. Then he set off jogging to catch up with the others.

* * *

They hadn't gone far. He found them contemplating a vertical rock wall. It was only about twenty feet high, but for them — for Yuri, at least — it was insurmountable. They had got themselves stuck in a cul-de-sac.

Magda hugged him with relief. 'We heard the shooting, and . . .'

'I'm fine. But we've got to keep moving. Their pals will have heard it, as well.'

Jake swung round, seeking a way out. Looking at the wall again, he knew they couldn't continue on the line they had been following. They had reached the end of it.

'We'd better head downhill,' he decided.

'No, Jake!' Yuri objected breathlessly. 'It is better to go up the hill.'

'What the hell are you talking about?' Jake snapped. 'That's too hard.'

Yuri shook his head. 'If we go up a short distance, we will come to a proper path, a good one. Down,' he said, motioning with both hands, 'will be very difficult. Also, they will see us if we go that way.'

'A path? What makes you say that?' Jake asked.

'I remember it.'

'You remember it? For God's sake, Yuri! You've never been here before.'

'But this I know,' Yuri said stubbornly. 'I remember from a map in Magda's flat. It is not far. Maybe thirty metres. We should go up there now.'

It seemed highly improbable. Jake turned to Magda.

'What do you think?' he asked her.

'I think we need to move, Jake. Now! I can hear them coming. We don't have time. I also believe Yuri. He did study my maps, and we know how good his memory is. We should try to find this path.'

Jake gave in. He was persuaded. It was worth trying. Anyway, path or not, if they headed uphill, the lie of the land meant they would soon be out of sight. Downhill, they would be visible all the way.

'Let's give it a go,' he said.

CHAPTER FIFTY-EIGHT

Magda led the way. Jake was behind Yuri, steadying him, helping him balance, and holding him when he was in danger of slipping and falling. The first ten metres or so, on steep and loose, gravelly ground, were the hardest. Then the slope eased, allowing them to stand upright and move without using their hands.

A few minutes more, and they hit the path. Surprisingly, it looked well used by something — people or animals, both perhaps. Jake gave Yuri a hug of appreciation and got a nervous smile in response.

Then they kept going, Magda still leading, Jake still the backmarker, glancing back over his shoulder even more often now. They might have won a few minutes, but the gunshots would have alerted the chasing pack. It wouldn't take long for the Russians to figure out what had happened. Then, with two of their men down, there was even less doubt about what would happen when they caught up.

And catch up they would, Jake knew. All they were doing by continuing to run was delaying the inevitable.

Yet hope hadn't died. Not quite. Unreasonable, unjustified hope was still alight. Either that or it was raw survival instinct. They were not dead yet, Jake reminded himself with grim determination.

Suddenly, there was a squawking noise from his earpiece, which in the mayhem of the last hour he had forgotten he was wearing.

'You should be able to hear us now,' he heard a familiar voice say, if a bit squeakily. 'Can you?'

Henderson! Astonished, Jake paused and pulled the earpiece out of his best ear to hear better. He listened, and he could hear it: Whump-whump-whump! Getting louder, getting nearer. It was a sound to make his heart lift.

Magda, too, had stopped and turned when she realised something was happening. He grinned, gave her a thumbs-up and waved her on.

'We're on an east–west path,' he said into his mic, as he reinserted the earpiece. 'We're making for an old house just off the main track up the hill. A couple of hundred yards to go.'

Henderson acknowledged. They pressed on. But not for long. On one of his backward glances, Jake spotted several figures on the path behind them. He grimaced. The Russians had probably split up, some going downhill and these few heading uphill — and getting it right. They were moving fast, jogging at a good pace, too good.

'Keep going!' he called to Magda, who had stopped again and was also looking back. 'I'll drop off in a minute and try to hold them up.'

The prospect was grim, but he refused to dwell on that now they had come so far. Just keep going, he told himself. Yard by yard, minute by minute. Something could still happen, could still turn up.

Moments later, it did. Two helicopters burst over the hilltop with a tremendous roar.

'Got you!' the voice in his ear announced. 'You're nearly there, Jake. And we're coming down for you.'

Thank God! he said to himself with inexpressible relief.

Then he turned and was very worried all over again as he looked back along the path. The gap was closing rapidly.

The Russians were really running now, racing hard. They had seen and appreciated the danger of external intervention and were not going to allow it to happen.

Jake wished he had hung on to both submachine guns instead of abandoning one. He wished now that he had more bullets with him for the Glock. He wished . . .

One of the choppers hung in the air above the path a little way ahead of them, close to a stone barn that Jake recognised from their visit the previous year. A crewman was standing in the open doorway, waving, beckoning, urging them on.

He heard a loudspeaker announcement from the second chopper, which had flown past them and was now hovering above the path, very close to the ground, a short distance behind him. He couldn't make it out, but it was very definitely a warning. The announcement was interrupted by a burst of heavy machinegun fire that made the gravity of the warning even clearer. Definitely not from sub-machineguns, Jake thought with enormous satisfaction.

Breathless, the three of them burst onto the rough grass area next to the now abandoned farm cottage. The man who had been waving them onwards launched himself on a rope out of the open doorway of the helicopter and descended fast.

Within seconds, Yuri and Magda were both scooped up and whisked away together. Jake flattened himself on the ground and stared back the way they had come, weapon in hand, no longer devoid of hope and ready to fight on.

It wasn't necessary. The tide had turned. More covering gunfire from the helicopter guarding the path had stopped the pursuit. No hazy figures firing weapons emerged from the cloud of dust now covering the path.

In seconds, the man from the first chopper was back, this time to take Jake away with him. It was over.

CHAPTER FIFTY-NINE

With Jake and his handler still swinging wildly from the rope, the helicopter rose and swept away, flying fast and low, heading for the eastern end of the Rocha da Pena, and the miles and miles of open fields beyond. They were winched up rapidly until welcoming hands could grab them and pull them inside the aircraft.

Jake was steered to a seat across the aisle from Magda and Yuri, who were both looking exhausted but happy beyond belief. Speech was impossible, given the usual noise level inside a helicopter, but he didn't mind that at all. He needed time to recover from the last few hectic minutes.

Magda leaned forward with a smile and squeezed his knee. He smiled back and nodded to her, and then to Yuri, getting a rare smile in return.

After that, he found he was sitting next to an also smiling Giles Henderson, who handed him headphones. It was smiles all round. For once, everybody was happy.

'What fun!' Henderson chortled when the headphones were in place. 'Well done, Jake. Very well done, indeed!'

For a moment, Jake felt like punching the smile off his face. But grace and the continuing sense of happiness led him to think better of it and keep his cool. Yet the desperate nature of their eleventh-hour rescue, as well as much of what had gone before, seemed to him to have been totally unnecessary.

He contented himself with saying, 'You left it a bit late, Sir Giles.'

Henderson nodded, apparently in agreement. 'Bureaucracy caused that, I'm sorry to say. The Portuguese are lovely people, and they're very ancient and valuable allies, of course, but they stick to the old ways when it comes to paperwork. It's why I'm here myself, actually. I came to try to expedite matters. Even now, though, we may not have every official permission needed for the operation.'

'Good to see you anyway,' Jake conceded, managing to overcome his reluctance to admit it.

Henderson grinned and patted him on the arm.

* * *

The helicopter flew them to a military airport a few miles outside Faro, possibly the one Henderson had originally had in mind. As he climbed out, Jake noted that the aircraft had no markings of any sort anywhere on its external surface. A true off-the-books mission, he concluded, wondering if that would have made it easier or harder to obtain the permissions Henderson had needed. The latter, probably. National sovereignty had to be respected, and indeed demanded it. Perhaps he ought to congratulate the boss, after all.

He looked around for the other helicopter, but it wasn't in sight. Possibly quarantined because it had opened fire. He knew how these things worked. Stupidly! Anything to satisfy the lawyers, of whom there were more than ever.

He, Magda and Yuri were gathered by several men in standard NATO military camouflage uniforms and hustled along a lengthy corridor in a two-storey brick building that was as functional and soulless as military structures usually were in Jake's experience. Henderson, accompanied by two minders — officially, close protection officers — followed at a gentler pace, no doubt with the respect due to his age and seniority.

The outcome was the same for them all. The entire party was taken to a room on the upper floor of the building, where there were sofas and coffee tables, as well as machines capable of dispensing a variety of drinks. Jake saw no sign of anybody who might have been a Portuguese national. So far as the host country was concerned, it looked as if none of this was happening, which was the sensible way to handle it. Henderson had obviously been able to cut through much of the bureaucracy, if not all of it.

Henderson's minders sorted out drinks for everyone. Then they discreetly withdrew from the room, no doubt to mount guard outside the door. The great man himself then welcomed the three of them, thanked them for enduring what had obviously been terrible hardships, and congratulated them wholeheartedly on their achievement in escaping such a resolute opposition. He made a particular point of addressing his remarks to Magda and Yuri, neither of whom had he ever met before.

Magda smiled and thanked him. Typically, Yuri looked bored. Jake had long since decided that was one of his ways of dealing with stress, fear and all other unpleasant events outside his control. At least he didn't give voice to what, no doubt, would be his very many reasons for dissatisfaction and grievance.

On the other hand, Jake thought, he wouldn't have minded hearing how Sir Giles dealt with the sort of Yuri-isms he himself had had to put up with over the past month. It might have been a rewarding learning experience.

Henderson did no more than nod pleasantly to Jake. Then he told the three of them that they should not regard this session as a debriefing. That would come later. For now, he just wanted them all to try to relax a little and begin to recover from their ordeal.

He glanced at his watch and added, 'In just a few minutes, we shall be boarding a plane that will fly us home. Mr

Bortsov, we will talk to you then about how you see your future, and where you wish to go.'

And that, Jake wasn't sorry to find, was that for the moment. Their long journey was over. The miles were done. They could sleep at last, at last.

CHAPTER SIXTY

In an early debriefing session, Henderson talked to the three of them together. It was an easy-going exchange intended to map out the chase across so much of Europe. Context, Henderson called it. And necessary. Maybe, Jake thought, but it was still painful to go through it all again.

At one point, he asked Henderson if he knew who had been coordinating the manhunt until General Blok had taken over.

'Ah!' Henderson said. 'Actually, we do. We have quite a good picture of that. Initially, it was Colonel Kozlov, who took over the relevant department of the GRU when General Blok retired a year or so ago. Then Blok was brought back to run things. We don't know why, but presumably someone — the president himself, probably — decided things were not going so well. By then, of course, Yuri, you had made good your escape and were running free.'

Yuri nodded. 'I quite liked Colonel Kozlov. He was kind to me, unlike General Blok.'

Henderson stared for a moment, unsure how to respond. Jake smiled and looked down. Kindness wouldn't be something much mentioned in departmental life under Sir Giles. The house culture, inevitably, was all about means and ends.

Probably not too dissimilar to the norm inside the equivalent Russian department.

Henderson recovered quickly enough and said smoothly, 'Then I'm sorry to have to tell you, Yuri, that Colonel Kozlov is no longer with us. He suffered a fatal accident while boarding a ferry from the island of Armona. He fell down a flight of steps, apparently, and broke his neck, poor chap.'

'But Blok was running things by then anyway,' Jake said.

'Yes. From Moscow. Not on the ground in Portugal, though.'

'Then who replaced Kozlov in the field?'

'No one. At least, no one of equivalent stature. The senior *Spetsnaz* officer in the group in Portugal has been running things on the ground, while liaising directly with Blok, of course.'

Jake nodded. It made sense. You didn't want an elderly desk officer getting in the way of men on the battlefield.

Yuri seemed troubled. In fact, he looked stunned.

'All right, Yuri?' Jake asked.

Yuri shook his head and reiterated that he had liked Kozlov. Then he added, 'Perhaps the *Spetsnaz* officer in charge is Sergeant Radowski?'

'Yes,' Henderson said. 'I believe that is so. Do you know him, too?'

'Slightly. And now I don't believe Colonel Kozlov's death was an accident.'

'Oh?' Henderson looked interested.

'I believe Blok will have ordered Kozlov's death, and this man, Radowski, is the one who will have killed him. He is close to Blok. They were in the North Caucasus together, and Blok has used him a lot.'

'We wondered about that,' Henderson said thoughtfully. 'Still, Kozlov's end makes a refreshing change from the unsavoury business of poisoning your colleagues and opponents, doesn't it?'

* * *

For the rest of the day, Yuri had little to say. Jake noticed that he spent a lot of time on the phone he had been given.

'Research,' Yuri said, when Jake asked him what he was doing.

'Research?'

Yuri nodded but didn't look up, let alone explain more.

Jake shrugged and left him to it. Something to do with his book, no doubt. And why not? They all needed something to do, some form of distraction therapy. Another day or two here — wherever it was — and he and Magda would be free to leave, he hoped. But poor Yuri had a lot more of this to look forward to. The rest of his life, perhaps, although Jake fervently hoped that wouldn't be the case.

Magda didn't take silence and a refusal to look up from a screen as an acceptable answer. Possibly, Jake thought, because she hadn't spent as much time with Yuri as he had. It made a difference.

'What are you researching, Yuri?' she asked.

Yuri uttered a great sigh. Whether one of relief, satisfaction or irritation, Jake couldn't tell. It was something different, though, he had to admit.

'Yuri?' Magda gently pressed.

'General Blok,' Yuri said, looking up at her.

'Oh?'

'I have been trying to find him.'

With a smile, Magda said, 'And have you done that?'

'Yes. Now I have.'

'So where is he?'

'In his office, sitting at his desk.'

'Which . . . ?'

'The same office, the same desk, in Moscow.'

Curious now, intrigued even, Jake said, 'How can you possibly . . . ?'

'Shut up, Jake,' Yuri said. 'I am thinking.'

Annoyed, Jake stood up, feeling like throwing a punch. Magda grabbed his arm hard and pulled him back down. He

202

glared at her. She made a gentle, soothing sound and shook her head.

Meanwhile, Yuri had begun tapping out something more on his phone.

'I should never have given him the damned thing,' Jake said quietly.

Again, Magda cautioned and quietened him with a forbidding look that couldn't be ignored.

'Ah!' Yuri said a moment later at a sudden indescribable, loud noise from his phone. He waved the phone in the air, as if frustrated beyond measure.

'Dead?' Jake asked with a sympathetic grin. 'It happens. Technology, eh?'

Yuri waved the phone some more and then seemed to give up on it. 'Dead!' he agreed, getting to his feet.

Then he left the room.

'Poor Yuri,' Magda said. 'After all the time he's spent on it, too.'

'I'll ask Henderson if a technician can take a look and see if it can be fixed,' Jake said. 'Otherwise, they'll just have to get him a new one. He can't be left with nothing to do, can he?'

'What did he mean, do you think, about finding General Blok?' Magda asked.

'No idea,' Jake said with a yawn, 'and I don't really care either. I've just about had enough of trying to work out Yuri's little mysteries. I'm ready to go home.'

'To which one, though?' Magda asked with a smile.

'I've had enough of hot weather, as well. Let's go to Northumberland and see how the new roof on the cottage is coping with hill rain.'

'Mm,' Magda said wistfully. 'I'd like that.'

'That's funny,' Jake said with a frown, having picked up the phone to examine it. 'The phone seems OK to me. I can't see what Yuri was on about.'

CHAPTER SIXTY-ONE

'I have some news that might interest you, Jake,' Sir Giles Henderson said. 'Mr Bortsov too, I'm sure, when I see him.'

Jake looked up from the newspaper he was reading and smiled to himself. He doubted very much that the news would interest either of them.

But he was wrong. Sir Giles's news was very interesting indeed.

'Moscow is having an extraordinarily bad run of luck,' Henderson said. 'We have just learned via intercepts that they have lost General Blok now. He's been killed. It's most extraordinary.'

'Blok?' Jake said, snapping awake. 'The man running the hunt for us?'

'The very one,' Sir Giles said with a look of bemusement.

'How did that happen? Did he fall down some steps, as well?'

'No, no. Something quite different. So far as we can make out, he was killed by a bomb explosion — in his own office, can you believe! Most extraordinary.'

That took Jake aback for a moment or two. Having absorbed the information, and thought about it, he said slowly, 'Yes, I can believe it, actually. Bombs can be detonated remotely, can't they?'

'Indeed, they can. We've moved on from Colonel Stauffenberg's day. Alas, he was born too soon. Had he known how to do it, Hitler wouldn't have—'

'By phone even?' Jake interrupted, declining to be distracted by a historical excursion to the Third Reich.

Sir Giles frowned now. 'What are you trying to tell me, Jake?'

'You don't really need to inform Yuri about Blok's death, Sir Giles. I believe he knows already. He may even have had something to do with it himself.'

* * *

Sir Giles went off immediately, looking for Yuri, but Jake got to him first.

'No comment,' Yuri said when Jake first asked him the question.

'Come on, Yuri! I know it was you. How did you manage it?'

'Hmm?'

'Surely they didn't train you in bomb warfare?'

It was a struggle, but the need to share what he knew, and perhaps to be congratulated for what he had done, was too strong to be resisted for long. Yuri gave in with a smile.

'Trained in bomb warfare? Of course not, Jake.'

'Well, then?'

Yuri shrugged modestly. 'I remember things. You know that. Things I read and see and hear. Files, technical reports, training courses for agents . . .'

'Even so?'

Yuri smiled again, taking pity on him. 'So I made a bomb and fitted it into his desk a long time ago, when I decided he wasn't being fair to me. Then he left, and Colonel Kozlov took over.'

'And you just left the bomb there?'

Yuri shrugged. 'Extracting it would have been difficult, dangerous even. And my life had become better. Not good, but better. So, yes, I left it.'

Jake was staggered. The man was incredible. The enormity of what he had done was breathtaking. Yet, to him, it was all very simple, and eminently reasonable.

'And you remembered it?'

'Of course. After Colonel Kozlov was murdered, as I believe, I thought of it again. First, though, I had to find out if General Blok was using his old office and his old desk. That took a little time.'

Didn't it just? Jake thought, marvelling. A whole bloody day nearly!

'Research on your phone, perhaps?'

'That was the difficult part,' Yuri said with a frown. 'It took me a long time to find and break into the internal viewing system — what you call CCTV, I believe?'

Jake nodded. 'And then you called the number — which you remembered, of course — that detonated the whole bloody thing?'

'Naturally,' Yuri agreed, looking and sounding remarkably chipper about it all.

'Well, I take my hat off to you, Yuri. You did it! Payback time, eh?'

'Yes,' Yuri agreed, smiling happily. 'Colonel Kozlov can rest in peace now.'

But can the rest of us, Jake wondered? He'd better warn Sir Giles Henderson to tread carefully and treat Yuri with respect — or else!

CHAPTER SIXTY-TWO

'I worry about Yuri,' Magda said, rather sadly. 'Where he'll end up, I mean.'

'Why's that?' Jake said.

'Well, I don't believe the Russians will stop hunting him. He knows too much. You're more aware of that than me, Jake.'

'True. And you're right. It will be hard to keep him safe in Oxford or Cambridge, or anywhere else in the UK, for that matter.'

'Oh, poor Yuri. Is it really as bad as that?'

'Yes, and no. Henderson is no fool. He'll soon come to that conclusion himself, once he's got what he wants out of him. Then he'll probably hand him over to the Americans.'

'They haven't been involved so far, have they?'

Jake smiled. 'Oh, I think they have. It was actually their operation originally, but they cocked it up. Their exfiltration team was assassinated in Slovakia. They were all killed. So the Americans have a score to settle. Henderson stepped in off his own bat when that happened and saved the day in an improvised, off-the-record op for which he had no approval whatsoever. He needed the month we gave him to get things sorted in London. Hence your new passport, in gratitude.

'The other thing is that those helicopters that came for us in the Algarve were not Henderson's to command. They were unmarked, but I believe they were American. The Yanks are the only people who could have mounted the mission to rescue us at such short notice and so effectively. Our lot are more cloak-and-dagger when it comes to intelligence missions. We can't put boots on the ground like the Americans can. We just don't have their resources. So, I'm sure Sir Giles will have done a deal with them and smoothed their collective ego. He'll have told them that in exchange for pulling us out of the fire, he would pass Yuri on to them in due course.'

Magda pondered for a moment. 'Is that going to be good for him, do you think?'

'For Yuri? Yes, I think it probably is. He'll have a better chance of staying alive in America than he would in Britain. We've struggled to keep Russian defectors alive in this country, as you may have noticed. The US is vastly bigger and less hidebound by legal rules than us. Also, their intelligence people have resources we can't match.'

Still pondering, Magda said, 'But will he be happy there, do you think?'

'Happy? Who knows?' Jake said, blowing out his cheeks. 'If they give him the facilities he needs to work on his book, he might be.'

'Facilities? What will he need for that?'

'Not much. A desk and chair, a bed, food, internet connection — and being kept alive! Oh, and a publisher at the end of the day. That should do it.'

CHAPTER SIXTY-THREE

'What about how they tracked us?' Jake asked. 'That's been doing my head in.'

Henderson shook his head. 'I'm not surprised. You had a terrible time in the Balkans and Italy, didn't you?'

'Not only there. Portugal was even worse. When we dug the pellet out of Yuri, we thought that would be it, but it wasn't. How did they continue to find us? Do we even know?'

'You were right, obviously, about the tracker beacon. For a time, after you removed it, they were stymied. Then they recovered and found another way.'

'I even wondered if they had inserted something in Bortsov's brain?'

'Nothing so picturesque, I'm afraid,' Henderson said with another shake of the head.

'Then what? Leaks?'

Again, Henderson said no. 'It looks as though they were able to hack into our computer systems and monitor both text and voice messaging. Our experts are currently looking into it further.'

'Well, that's not good enough! I'm not having that. Somebody is to blame. Who is it?'

'Me, I'm afraid. I had a rescue mission to organise in a hurry, and I didn't know our systems had been compromised.'

Jake pushed his chair back violently, in anger and frustration.

'If I hadn't pulled my finger out, Jake, there would have been no rescue mission. You would have perished on that hillside. Sometimes, we just have to take risks.'

Jake brought his chair back down on to four legs, his anger evaporating. The voice of reason had prevailed.

'Well, I'll tell you this,' he said slowly. 'The department isn't fit to look after Yuri. You need to put him in safer hands. He deserves nothing less.'

'Just so,' Henderson admitted. 'And I have already spoken to our friends across the pond about that.'

Jake tried not to wince at the archaic slang reference to the US and carried on.

'Something else I want to tell you is that you need to look after him for your own personal sake. Don't take Yuri for granted. Remember General Blok — and be warned!'

* * *

'Where are you taking him, anyway?' Jake asked. 'Where's he going to end up?'

'That is yet to be decided.'

Jake nodded. He knew what that meant. It meant it was outside Henderson's control, as well as outside Yuri's.

'Oxford, maybe? Cambridge? Or somewhere smaller, perhaps, like Exeter or Durham?'

'I wish I could tell you, Jake. There's a lot of sorting out to do before his destination is decided.'

Jake felt more than a little sorry for Yuri, which earlier in their relationship would have been very unlikely. Henderson presumably meant that there were to be many, many interrogation sessions ahead while they wrung out of Yuri everything they could.

'Initially, you know, he assumed I was CIA. He thought he was going to the States.'

'Really?'

Which seemed to mean that wasn't going to happen now, or not in the immediate future, at least.

'What I do know, Jake, is that you did extraordinarily well to bring him all that way, and to look after him so well. An extraordinary achievement. It really is appreciated.'

'It was touch-and-go at times,' Jake admitted. 'But I had a lot of help.'

'Your partner?'

'Magda, yes.'

'Her part in all this is also acknowledged. You make a good team.'

'So, she's off the hook now?'

'Of course.' Henderson smiled. 'She was never really on it. I'm sure you knew that all along?'

Jake smiled, trying hard to be just as equivocal. He wasn't at all sure that he did know that, and it was good to have the assurance.

'And she'll get a new passport?'

'I have it with me. I shall give it to her as soon as we're finished here.'

'Thank you.'

'The least I could do.'

It was, too, Jake thought. But at least it was done. They didn't need to worry anymore about that.

'Tell me, Jake. How did you find Mr Bortsov, in a personal sense?'

Jake smiled inwardly. He knew Henderson had already seen quite a bit of Yuri since they had all been back in the UK.

'A bit difficult at first, if I'm being honest. You don't have a normal relationship with him. You can't. He's a very special sort of person.'

'In what way?'

'Well . . . I don't know where to start. Egotistical, remote, self-centred . . . If you spend time with him, you'll soon find out what I mean. But he has his good points as well, of course, and you find them as you get to know him. He's had a rotten time of it. Frustrated, and living in fear. He's very much a loner, too. We have to remember that. Also, Magda believes he's autistic. Put all that together and . . .'

'Ah!' Henderson nodded with apparent understanding.

'That means something to you? The autism part, perhaps?'

'Quite a lot, actually. It explains his extraordinary capabilities. He really is a very valuable asset.'

Jake couldn't let that go unchallenged. 'No doubt,' he said, 'but he's also a human being, a decent and special one. We grew fonder of him as we got to know him better. My advice would be to go easy with him. And, as I've already told you, keep in mind what happened to General Blok.'

'Point taken,' Henderson said with a chuckle. 'Don't worry. He'll be well looked after.'

'By the way, do you know he's writing a book, which he regards as his life's work?'

Looking intrigued, as well he might, Henderson shook his head.

'So you don't know what his life's work is about?'

Again, Henderson shook his head.

'The Battle of Kursk.'

'The what?' Henderson looked perplexed for a moment. Then, plain puzzled. 'Not the tank battle in . . . ?'

'The Great Patriotic War, as they call it, yes. He's writing about it.'

'Good heavens! What's he done with the manuscript? He didn't have it with him.'

'It's in his head. He's writing it in his head.'

'Ah!' Henderson said, a faraway look coming into his eyes. After a few moments, he added, 'His memory must be even more exceptional than I had thought.'

'It's certainly that, all right.'

'Do you happen to know why he is doing that?'

'Not really. Kursk is his home town, of course. But my guess, from bits I picked up along the way, is that Bortsov and Blok antecedents may well have encountered one another as adversaries during that encounter, regardless of whether or not they wore the same uniform.

'Yuri said at one point in our journey that he wanted to put right a wrong that had been done, a family member unjustly executed during the battle. I don't know any details, but I believe that explains his motivation for the book, and also Blok's demise.'

'Really? How interesting.'

After a little reflection, Sir Giles said, 'In the end, of course, Yuri took care of it, in his own way, whatever it may have been. Perhaps he doesn't need to finish the book now?'

'Oh, I think he does,' Jake said decisively. 'And I believe he will.'

On that note, he took his leave, not exactly triumphant at knowing more than Sir Giles Henderson for once, but quietly pleased all the same.

CHAPTER SIXTY-FOUR

'I hope to see your book when it's finished,' Jake said.

'Oh, yes! You will,' Yuri said with a warm smile. 'It will be everywhere, thanks to Mr Henderson. He is a real English gentleman. He understands how important it is to have a detailed and correct account of important moments in history. Unfortunately, people in my own country did not agree. They just wanted me to work on things that matter to them, but not to me.'

Jake wondered for a moment how much of a gentleman Giles Henderson really was, and how much he simply wanted to find out what Yuri knew about Russian Intelligence operations and infrastructure. Pass, he thought. I'll never know.

'Where will you go now, Yuri? Do you know?'

'I know only that it will be a small city that is very quiet and has a big library.'

Oxford and Cambridge might not quite fit that picture, Jake thought, as he'd suggested to Magda. He wondered if Henderson had somewhere like Durham or Exeter in mind instead. Or if it would turn out to be the Davis campus of the University of California. Or even Saint John or Fredericton in New Brunswick, Canada.

Somewhere like the latter would be even better. Easier to arrange. And quieter, certainly. Very quiet, in fact. He smiled at the thought. Would it match Yuri's expectations of life in the West? Perhaps not. Probably nowhere would.

'I hope you will be happy, wherever it is,' Magda contributed. 'After all that's happened to you, you deserve to be.'

'Yes,' Yuri said earnestly. 'You are right, Magda. And I hope you and Jake will be happy too. You have both been very kind to me.' Just as it seemed he had finished, he added, 'Some of the time, at least.'

Was that a joke? Jake wasn't sure. As ever with Yuri, it was hard to tell.

Then they shook hands and said their goodbyes, and Yuri walked over to the waiting official Jaguar to be whisked away to . . . somewhere.

THE END

Thank you for reading this book.

If you enjoyed it please leave feedback on Amazon or Goodreads, and if there is anything we missed or you have a question about, then please get in touch. We appreciate you choosing our book.

Founded in 2014 in Shoreditch, London, we at Joffe Books pride ourselves on our history of innovative publishing. We were thrilled to be shortlisted for Independent Publisher of the Year at the British Book Awards.

www.joffebooks.com

We're very grateful to eagle-eyed readers who take the time to contact us. Please send any errors you find to corrections@joffebooks.com. We'll get them fixed ASAP.